Why

by
Patricia Barnes

AuthorHouse™ UK Ltd.
500 Avebury Boulevard
Central Milton Keynes, MK9 2BE
www.authorhouse.co.uk
Phone: 08001974150

© 2009 Patricia Barnes. All rights reserved.

No part of this book may be reproduced, stored in a retrieval system, or transmitted by any means without the written permission of the author.

First published by AuthorHouse 4/22/2009

ISBN: 978-1-4389-4363-3 (sc)

This book is printed on acid-free paper.

CHAPTER 1

Savannah returned to the Island

At a distance of perhaps two hundred and fifty feet from the ancient silk cotton tree, I stood on the edge of what were once magnificently kept gardens. Beyond where I stood inconsolably looking upon the devastation of my childhood home, there was a separate garden my grandmother had tended with the utmost care. This was her private space where she could escape from the demands of her huge family. In order to make this space perfect for Grandma, Uncle Arnold had built his mother the most exquisite summer house in the centre of the garden. Flowers, plants, shrubs, and trees of every type imaginable were planted there. These became as much a part of my family's history as I was myself. As a child, I was familiar with the terrifying fable that surrounded the silk cotton tree. The older members of my family and the community related various legends to us children. Whether these legends were used as a deterrent, I never knew. What I did know, however, was that in spite of the infamous legend the silk cotton trees on the island attracted, I was never afraid of this particular tree.

By the time I was born, the silk cotton tree behind our family home had grown into a gigantic monster. Its branches stretched like tentacles to enslave the other trees in an unholy marriage of supremacy. Its dominance had earned the tree iconic status. People came from far and near to gaze up at the monster tree that Fredrick Holness, my great-grandfather, had planted in the seventeenth century when he first acquired the land, which he named Peaceful View. Instinctively my eyes travelled back to the silk cotton tree, its once-obstinate branches now burnt and its leaves withered and blackened by what must have been an inferno. Flames of intense heat had transformed everything. Now the silk cotton tree's future mirrored my own. Uncertainty and a mound of grey-black ruins were all that remained of my inheritance.

Consumed with grief at the sight of the ruins of a house so precious to me, I failed to notice that a shadowy figure had appeared from somewhere beyond the smoke and was standing just behind me. Laden with all manner of woes, I sighed and inhaled a lungful of smoke-filled air. So thoroughly immersed in the scenes of devastation around me, my obsessive memories soon carried me back to the safety of the house's old whitewashed walls; and its undisturbed peace. My memories caused my heart to ache as if broken in two, my head pounded, and tears streamed from my eyes from both hopelessness and smoke. The desolation around me forced memories past and present, which in turn threatened to squeeze the very life from me. All was lost; there were no treasured photographs hanging from the walls, no cherished pieces of furniture, and no belongings – just grey-black ashes and an empty shell.

I had arrived unannounced to surprise my uncle, but he was nowhere to be seen.

I stood alone, not knowing what to do or where to turn. I had no other close family member alive on the island; my uncle was all I had left. My grandparents, aunts, and uncles were long dead, and with no one to explain the devastation around me. I wished with all my heart, that I was back in the safety of my neat little flat in England, surrounded by the lonely emptiness of the life I had grown accustomed to. Burning smells of hundreds of years of my family's history smouldered on relentlessly behind me. I closed my eyes, hoping my pain would be blotted out. I tried to imagine smells of the sweet country air I used to love as a child, but that too became wormwood to my senses. I smelt and felt poison infiltrating my bloodstream; feelings of venomous hate for the person or persons responsible for the carnage behind me, trickled through my veins. I became aware of a plan of revenge taking shape in my head.

In the meantime, a long thin hand with clawlike, smoke-blackened fingernails hovered above me. Suddenly, it came to rest on my left shoulder. My heart lurched and my legs threatened to collapse from beneath me. Startled, I looked up into a careworn face with vacant chestnut eyes. The man's long beard had turned shades of copper, yellowish white and dirty brown. The hair on his head matched his beard perfectly and was equally tangled. His complexion varied from shades of olive to sun-baked brown. His clothes were clean but hung loosely from his thin body. I looked deep into the man's eyes, and he held my gaze. I could swear I saw flickers of recognition, yet I wasn't certain. Though his face reflected the hardship, he appeared to have suffered; the heart-shaped mouth and haunting chestnut eyes struck a memory somewhere in my subconscious. My mind searched for memories of him, but I could not put a name to this hauntingly eccentric creature.

His penetrating eyes seemed to be turning my soul inside out, and I desperately wanted to move away from him. His hand on my shoulder and his penetrating stare heightened my sense of fear and panic surrounded me. I felt like an animal caught in a trap and my body grew tensed with fear. I wanted to escape from him, but my legs were rooted to the spot. Then, as if he could sense my fear and confusion, his expressionless face unexpectedly changed. The very corners of his eyes creased as they were touched by the faintest smile. The rest of his face remained unaltered – remote and unreadable.

"Are you afraid of me... Vannah?" he asked with a slight tilt of his head to one side. My mind, along with the charred remains around me, began to spin. As far as my memory served me, only one person called me by the name Vannah, and that person was dead. I averted my eyes from his expressionless face, not knowing whether to turn and run or to simply throw myself upon the smouldering ashes of my childhood home.

I opened my mouth to speak, but not a sound bubbled forth. Ever so cautiously, I lifted the man's hand from my shoulder. I let go of his hand, and it fell lifeless at his side, as though it was not a part of his body. I already felt numb and panic-stricken, and new feelings of danger rendered me speechless. I began to back away from him, then I turned and ran. I came to a stop in the family's cemetery. I threw myself upon what I recognised as my grandmother's tomb, and I dissolved into hysterical weeping.

"Why? Why, dear God… why?" I sobbed. Moments later a shrilling scream pierced through the silence of the night and reverberated through the darkness of the surrounding hills.

CHAPTER 2

I must have sobbed myself to sleep I thought when I finally sat up and looked up at the darkened sky. My tears had dried up, and my heartbeat had settled back to its usual rhythm. The smells of smouldering wood still filled the air, and for a moment, I was brought back to the horrible present. I hung my head not knowing what to do. Then, as if a hand had been placed beneath my chin, my head slowly began to rise. In the distance, the blurred image of my grandmother appeared. I fancied I heard her voice calling me, "Savannah, will you come here please?" Moodily, I stared into the pits of my heart and a searing pain pulled me, as it always did, to a time when life was safe and the happy, carefree laughter of my huge extended family could be heard drifting on the gentle breeze. My mind's eye began to turn back the pages of my childhood memories, and I became a child again. Another episode in the conflict of wills between my grandmother and me ensued.

A Childhood Memory

I closed my eyes tightly and saw myself sitting on the wide windowsill in my bedroom. It was a chilly morning, for it had rained the night before. My nightgown was tucked snugly over my legs and drawn under my feet. A lavender bed jacket my cousin Etta made for me at her needlework classes was wrapped around my shoulders. I sat waiting to feel the first warm rays of the sun through the window. It was Sunday – a day for worshipping God. Grandma's voice drifted in under my bedroom door as she exercised her vocal cords in anticipation of her usual front-row seat in church. It wasn't Easter, but Grandma was humming a hymn - traditionally sung at that time. I cocked my ear, listening to Grandma's pretty voice. "Glory Be To Jesus." Grandma sang the words of the song one minute, then hummed them the next. I began to hum along too as I waited for the sun to appear. Whisky, my jet black dog, crept out from under my bed and began stretching himself.

Whisky's sharp front paws slid purposefully along the waxed floor, and I cringed, hoping his nails wouldn't penetrate the polish again. Any more scratches on the floor and my guilty secret would be out. Whisky bit on his tail, spinning around as he always did whenever anyone sang and, in particular, when Aunt Eva sang in her horrendous tone-deaf voice. People often plugged their ear with their fingers and begged to be spared from another attack of her dreadful voice. The poor animals on the farm would break into frenzied dance, and the beautiful birds nesting in the hills would flap their wings in distress and take flight.

Whisky whimpered and then jumped up onto the blanket box beneath the window, and then up onto the windowsill to join me. He placed a paw on my knee and searched my face for approval, for he wanted to sit on my lap.

"Oh… Whisky, my feet are cold. Sit there until the sun comes up. All right?" I said, patting his head and giving him a little scratch to keep him quiet. Satisfied, he rested his head on my knees and looked attentively up at me.

"Good doggie. Quiet now, or Grandma will catch you and we'll both be in trouble. You've never been in my room, and I have never taken you into the house either. It's our secret," I whispered into the furry pink softness of Whisky's ears. He leaned his head to one side, his pointed ears stood up, and, the conspirators that we were, we came to a silent agreement.

"You are the smartest dog in the whole wide world, Whisky. I'm glad you're mine. You understand everything I say to you. Do you know Grandma says you are more handsome than Aunt Rebecca's husband? She says Dick's a philistine and a heathen. I don't know why she calls him by so many names. He should have three names like everyone else. I don't mind him though, for he's funny." I giggled as I thought of the peculiar things Dick said and did. "Look, here it comes." I pointed excitedly towards the mountains in the far distance. Like me, the sky over the hills had waited in anticipation - drawing familiar patterns across the clouds, in varying shades of orange. The outer edges of the clouds, were touched with the faintest traces of baby pink shadows. Finally, the sun climbed slowly through the clouds, its circle of light spread like a huge umbrella over Peaceful View casting distorted shadows on the vegetation down below. As nature's hand gently pushed the big orange ball up through the clouds, animals, birds, and insects stirred from their sleepy dreams. Then, like the warmth of a hug, the sunrays kissed the dew-covered earth, and everything that had slept soundly awakened to its warm glow.

I adored nature, and my eager eyes keenly followed the sunrays as they travelled over the silvery dew on the leaves and grass. In awe, I watched as the dew on the vegetation began to vaporise like magic. Pockets of steam rose in one place after another. Sleepy flower petals unfolded, and leaves began to glisten on the tops of the hills. I sighed like an old woman as the thought of another Sunday in church crept into my head. I dreaded the fearsome sermons of Pastor Mac Farlane and hated going to church. His cold blue eyes never failed to home in on me as I fidgeted on the iron-hard wooden bench beside Grandma. I secretly held the opinion that Pastor Mac, as most called him, was Lucifer himself. I feared him as much as I feared his fire-and-brimstone sermons. I began to think of an ailment I could conjure up! I'd have to convince Grandma yet again that I wasn't well enough to go to church.

I'd had stomach cramp three weeks ago, a headache the week after that, and last week, I'd suffered nausea on the way to church and was sent home. I had to come up with something new. I began to think of a way out.

"Glory Be To Jesus. Hum, hum," Grandma sang as she did her usual rounds of knuckle rapping against bedroom doors to wake everyone up. "Rise and shine now," she said between singing and humming. Her voice was getting ever closer to my bedroom door as she climbed the stairs with determination. Sing... hum... sing... hum... then a brisk knock on a door along the way.

"Rise and shine now, everyone," Grandma said, as she lingered, waiting to hear sounds of life from the other side of each door. Then, all too soon, Grandma's footsteps came to a stop outside my bedroom door! I screwed up my face and narrowed my eyes. Twisting my mouth to one side, I waited. Knock! Knock! Grandma rapped on my door!

"Savannah Hanson, are you up? Are you awake? Rise and shine now."

Grandma's brusque Sunday-morning voice crept under the door and penetrated the walls around me. I covered my ears with my hands, sucked in my breath, and made a clicking noise with my tongue. I peered at Whisky through my fingers, rolled my eyeballs, and mocked my grandmother's words.

"Rise and shine. Rise and shine. I don't want to rise and shine, and I don't want to go to church either," I said, screwing up my face again, in distaste at the thought of going to church. I had been told by Pastor Mac a few weeks earlier that I was doomed to go to hell.

"There are two types of people in this world: those going nowhere and those going somewhere. You, my child, are an exception. There is only one destination for you, and that is hell!"

At the time, shivers of terror had run through me like the hot coco Grandma gave us at bedtime. Being so very young at the time, my only reaction to Pastor Mac's proclamation was fear! I soon developed a dread of hot coco, Pastor Mac, and his sermons, not to mention the Anglican church. I certainly did not want to be reminded of my dreaded fate.

I had no intention of going back to church. And anyway, what was the point if God wasn't going to save me from the devil he created in the first place? I reasoned. I had gone to Dick and related what the cold-hearted Pastor Mac had told me. Dick and me had discussed this and he had said.

"This church-going business was all poppycock. Churches are evil, cold places, full of hypocrites and money-grabbing so-called holy men who are dressed up like evil warriors. What man of God would say such terrible things to an eight-year-old child, I ask you?"

I had admitted to Dick, I hated Pastor Mac's eyes and the things he said from the pulpit. His devilish gown too was frightening, and I often imagined I saw two horns growing out of his head.

"Women only went to church for a dress rehearsal to compete and compare with each other, and men only went to keep their wives quiet or because they were looking at the women to see which ones they could tempt away from their husbands," Dick had said, adding that Pastor Mac was no different. "I have seen the way that charlatan looked at the ladies. That's the reason I banned Becky from going to church."

I heaved a sigh as Grandma's voice bombarded my brain again.

"I heard you mocking, Savannah Hanson! Have you said your prayers yet?" Grandma's tone wasn't a questioning one; it was a commanding one now.

"No, Gr-Grandma," I answered awkwardly. "Fiddlesticks! I can't even whisper. Grandma hears every word. Maybe she's living in my head!" I mimed to Whisky.

"And why not, may I ask? You haven't forgotten the words yet again, have you? I am coming in. You have enough time to get down from the windowsill. Get down on your knees ready for prayers."

I grumbled under my breath as I slid down off the windowsill like an anxious lizard. "Quickly...." I whispered to Whisky, shoving him along the floor back under my bed. I fell to my knees with my palms together and my eyes half shut. The door opened and Grandma entered.

"Well done, Savannah. See how easy it is to be obedient? Now... let's see. Why don't you start by thanking God for that beautiful sunrise you've just watched?" Grandma said, with eyes that leap out of her head as they surveyed the mess I had managed to create overnight. On the floor in the far side of my bedroom, were the previous day's contents from my dungaree pockets. My bed was a mixture of grass seeds, dried leaves, twigs, shells, plum seeds, pebbles for my catapult, and the remains of nightingales' eggshells. My favourite pastime was bird watching on Peaceful View and running naked through fields of corn, long grass, or the meadow below Aunt Rebecca and Dick's house. Bobby, my cousin and I had been watching a nightingale nest for weeks until the eggs had hatched into three chicks.

But of all the unthinkable things I often collected or did, the most offensive to Grandma, were the unmistakable black hair that belonged to my dog Whisky, clinging to my bed linen! A dog is loved and cared for but has its place and that was outside. Whisky had a doghouse, and Grandma could not understand my need to smuggle him and other animals into the house at every opportunity.

"Wow! Grandma's a witch! She sees everything even behind locked doors. How did she know I was watching the sunrise? Oh dear, what next?" I whispered to myself. Grandma continued to look in every corner of my room as if she had lost something. Barely stopping to take a breath she continued.

"Thank God for allowing you to see another day. Thank him for your family. Pray for others in the world and ask for his blessings and forgiveness. You need a lot more -, than the rest of us! By the way… you wouldn't be hiding anything in here that you shouldn't, would you, Savannah?" Grandma asked, raising one eyebrow knowingly as she leaned over to pull on one of my plaits.

"No… ooo… Grandma," I lied.

I had meant to tidy up the mess I had made but had got carried away watching the sunrise. Fleetingly, I saw Grandma's eyes pass over my bed! She was bent over the chest of drawers looking through the drawers. I could scarcely keep up with her movements as she busied herself tidying up. Cupboards and drawers were opened and slammed shut; curtains were pulled away from the windows. A whoosh of cold air wafted into the room as Grandma flung all the windows wide open. I shivered and began my prayers in earnest. I needed to distract Grandma and would have to add a silent footnote to my prayers. I dared not say this out loud. I began to pray.

"Now I wake and see the light. God has kept me through the night. Make me good, oh Lord, I pray, as from my bed I rise. Make all that I do and say be precious in your sight. Gentle Jesus, meek and mild, look upon this little child. Please bless all the people I love and look after everyone in the world too," I said. And then, in my mind, I added, "Please, God and the angels, make me have a bellyache this morning because I don't want to go to church. Pastor Mac preaches hellfire and brimstones. It scares me! If you can't give me a bellyache, then please let Grandma put out my new pink dress and matching hat. I will go to church if she does. Oh, I promise to be on my best behaviour too.

Why

Honest! Please don't let Grandma see the mess I've made. And please don't let her have to spank me this morning. Amen. I've finished my prayers, Grandma."

I grinned, hoping my prayers were enough for the mess I had made before going to bed the night before. And that Grandma wouldn't make me say my prayers all over again.

"Amen."

Grandma's voice drifted out from one of the cupboards. Then, as if led by some secret force, she appeared on the other side of my bed.

"Hum... hum. Glory Be To Jesus."

Grandma sang and then hummed as she moved briskly around my bed. She tugged crossly at the sheets and brushed at the bedcovers with furious strokes of her hand. Then she swiped viciously at Whisky's tufts of black hairs. Finally, she gave up and dragged the sheets off my bed. I watched as she marched over to the open window where she shook them without mercy. I looked on between the gaps in my fingers not daring to speak.

Back to the bed again, Grandma thumped my pillows harder than usual. She whizzed around my bed tugging at the sheets, and tucked them tightly under the mattress. When she was satisfied all signs of debris, dog hairs and wrinkles had been smoothed out with sweeping strokes of her hands -she stepped back and folded her arms. This lasted only a few seconds. It seemed a thought had popped into her head for she studied me with her silvery grey eyes. I held my breath. Grandma walked towards the cupboard where my best clothes hung in neat rows. She opened the door and reached inside. I took my hand away from my eyes. My face dropped - to my horror, she took the lilac dress I hated from the cupboard. Now she placed the frilly frothiness on the peg behind my bedroom door.

I stared at the dress, mortified, speechless. Neither God nor the angels had heard my prayers let alone answered them. The thought of wearing the dress made me want to run away and never be found again. I loved the lilac colour of the dress but hated the silly frilly frothiness around my legs. The big bow Grandma tied with the ribbons at the back of my waist made the other children tease me and call me Fairy Nancy. A pair of khaki dungarees would have been just fine. The sound of Grandma's voice disturbed my thoughts. Her authoritative words spilled from her lips like a tune from one of the hymns with which she often filled the house in the mornings. It was going to be another battle between me and Grandma, and the day had only just started!

"Fiddlesticks!" I whispered, under my exasperated breath.

I was half listening to Grandma's instructions and half planning my escape.

"You've watched me do this enough times, Savannah. Soon you will do this for yourself. Now go to your drawers. Fetch a pair of white socks, two white ribbons, and a pair of white pants and lay them out on your bed, please," Grandma ordered as she walked towards the lilac dress! Taking the dress down from the peg, Grandma laid it against the pillows on my now neatly arranged bed. She tugged lightly on the underskirt of crinoline and frothy lace. Smoothed her hand along the folds of the gathered skirt then she straightened the ribbons that tied into a bow at the back of the dress. She stepped back to admire the dress.

"I do so love to see you wearing this dress, Savannah. It makes you look like a little angel! It's a pity you can't behave like one, though!" Grandma said, giving my ear a tug.

"Ooooo… ooch. That hurt," I cried.

A mixture of bad temper and ungodly thoughts swirled inside my head now. I stamped my foot to show my determination.

"I won't wear that dress. I hate it! I'll be teased. I feel like a dumb fairy in it. I'll cut it to shreds," I screamed as I moved closer to the window for it was going to be my escape route.

"Savannah, I dare you to repeat what you've just said. I'm sure I did not hear you clearly!" Grandma said, spinning round to face me.

Her grey eyes had grown as dark as a stormy night. They appeared huge. Her jaws dropped, and she seemed to have forgotten to close her mouth. She picked up a slipper, and I knew I was about to get a thrashing. I glared defiantly at her anyhow and repeated my threat.

"I will cut it to sheds, if you make me wear it again. I hate that stupid dress."

I stamped my foot again just to make sure Grandma got the point. She made a sudden dash towards me, and I darted under the bed. There, I wedged myself between Whisky and the wall.

"Get out this minute, Savannah Hanson. That's an order."

Grandma's face loomed under the fringed edges of the throw on my bed. I started giggling because the fringes made Grandma's face look like one of the lampshades in the hall downstairs. My giggling only served to make Grandma angrier. She saw it as another act of defiance. Then she caught sight of Whisky and all hell broke loose!

"I've had enough of your behaviour, Savannah Hanson. Your tantrums get worse by the day. I will not tolerate this any longer, do you hear? Whatever happened to that sweet, placid child I once knew?"

Grandma wagged a finger at me and tried to pull me out from under the bed. Rebelliously, I shuffled further away from her grasp.

"I have told you time and again, animals are not allowed in the house and certainly not near or under beds. It's unhygienic. Get out this minute." Grandma's hand snatched at my legs, and I kicked out in fury. She turned to Whisky and shrieked, "Come here, Whisky. You know the rules and so does your badly-behaved owner. Out you come this minute!"

Unlike me, who had no time for Grandma's rules, Whisky shuffled out from underneath the bed and looked back at me with a sorry look on his faithful old face.

"Don't worry, Whisky. Grandma's not fast enough. She won't catch me. Meet you later," I whispered, hoping Grandma hadn't heard me!

Whisky sat by Grandma's feet, head bowed low in shame. He was a very proud dog but was gentle and obedient. Unfortunately, he was often in trouble, given that I was his owner. Unlike me who'd throw tantrums and run naked through the bush, Whisky would accept his punishment with dignity. He would have to spend the day, or at least a part of it, at Grandma's side. He whimpered and licked Grandma's leg as he sat obediently waiting to be ordered out. I hoped with all my heart, Grandma would not lock him in the doghouse. Whisky hated that more than anything. I would try not to worry too much for with Uncle Daniel's help, we would be re-united in no time. I listened as Grandma ordered Whisky out of the room.

"Get out. Gooood dog. Out. Out."

A stern finger pointed Whisky to the opened door! He turned around and disappeared down the stairs.

Grandma stood in the doorway and said, "I'll be back, Savannah. I am going to teach you a lesson – a lesson in good behaviour."

The door slammed and the key turned in the lock. Grandma stalked off behind Whisky, muttering to herself. I listened as her footsteps ebbed away down the stairs. I crawled out from underneath my bed and snatched up the hated dress. I jumped up on to the windowsill and climbed out through the window. The big silk cotton tree just outside my bedroom window welcomed me into its branches. Legend had it that all silk cotton trees were haunted by witches and ghosts; dreadful things are supposed to happen in the dead of night beneath their shadows. It was widely believed that if one was caught beneath the shadows of a silk cotton tree at noon or at midnight, that person would die shortly thereafter. Dick had told me this legend was poppycock. I believed everything Dick told me.

CHAPTER 3

I must have been blessed with additional lives for whatever secrets or legends the silk cotton tree held – I cared not. It was quite unlike other trees on Peaceful View, and its branches were considered to be as obstinate as I was. Whether the tree had grown before the house was built or the house was built before the tree had grown, no one could remember. Grandpa's great grandfather, Fredrick, built the house in the seventeenth century on ten acres of land he had acquired in a then-unpopulated area of the island. Fredrick Holness had arrived on the island as an overseer of a plantation where some of my ancestors were kept as slaves. I knew nothing much about him except he hailed from Kent in England. Over the years, prosperity had seen Fredrick's ten acres of land grow into two hundred acres of prime farmland. By the time Grandpa had inherited the property from his mother, Molly; the silk cotton tree had grown taller than the house and was threatening to destroy it with its giant limbs. The offending limbs had been cut back, and, later, a platform was built beneath one of the limbs. A tree house and an aviary had been built on top of the platform. It was to prevent my frequent disappearance, after Grandpa's death.

I edged my way along its branches over the top of the tree house, and the avery and disappeared into the tree's mysterious clutches like a slippery snake. I planned to give the dress to my cousin Lilly. We often met on the other side of the twin hills that separated Peaceful View from Lilly's grandmother's land. Aunt Rhonda, Lilly's grandmother, was Grandma's close relative but some sort of feud existed between those descendants of the Mac Dermot, and the Rochester's, the Duncan's and the Holness. I had no idea what the trouble was. It was something that had happened before I was born and was never spoken about in my presence. However, a distinct frost existed between Grandma and Aunt Rhonda. But there was a frost between Aunt Rhonda and the whole world. She was a cantankerous woman and she hated us children, especially me, because I always answered her back. The feeling between us was a mutual one for I disliked her like the devil disliked holy water.

****

When I finally rose to my feet, spent and exhausted, I looked around for signs of the man but he was gone. He had disappeared as mysteriously as he had appeared. I was alone in the darkness and I soon felt a strange foreboding. The blood in my body chilled like nothing I had ever felt before and I sensed danger. I shivered and jumped to my feet. I had to find him but did not know where to look. I decided to go back to the edge of the garden from where he had mysteriously appeared. I'd forgotten how suddenly darkness descended on the island. In no time, it was pitch-black. With creepy shadows for company, I stumbled along what I hoped was the same path I had run down earlier. I could not see clearly, but fear drove me along anyhow. I had to face him - I had to know the truth for my gut feelings told me that the fire was no accident.

It was time to face the unknown. I moved closer towards the area of the garden where the summer house used to be. I believed he was hiding there. I prayed feverishly for God to remove all feelings of fear from my heart, whilst I searched my memory for clues in Uncle Daniel's letters to me. Thankfully, I noticed a faint light between the trees ahead. I had no choice but to walk towards the light - stumbling as I went. My heartbeat accelerated thunderously as I drew closer to the light I had been following. The light moved! There was no doubt a shadow had passed before it. I hesitated and then groped around for something to defend myself with. I found a clump of wood and clutched on to it for dear life. Then, to calm myself, I decided it might just have been the breeze that had caused the light to move. Gingerly I continued forward, feeling my way through the darkness.

All too soon I came upon him. I stopped abruptly and almost toppled forward. My body shuddered as if in great pain. I felt cold and afraid – afraid of him, afraid of the dark, and afraid of what lay ahead of me.

"Vannah," he called, "don't be afraid. Come."

The solitary figure of the man appeared from the shadow and the smoke and stood holding up a storm lantern in his hand. To the left of him, I saw the little summer house.

"I thought you might not remember much about the old place. I lit the lantern and hung it up there for you," he said, pointing to the lantern.

He reached up and touched a leafless branch above his head. I faltered and my knees buckled. I had wanted to find him, but now I had no idea what to do next.

"I hoped that you'd see the light through the trees and follow it. Don't be afraid of me, Vannah. I won't harm you. Come," he said, hanging up the lantern on the branch he had pointed out moments earlier. He extended both his arms towards me. "Come to me, Vannah… please."

A lump wedged itself in my throat, and I swallowed to ward off my tears; his beseeching voice stabbed at my overburdened heart and I wondered what to do. He had called me Vannah! Only one person used to call me by that name. That person was Dick, and he had died years earlier. Who, I asked myself, was this strange and desolate-looking man? He walked up to the door of the summer house and pushed it open. It swung creepily back on its hinges, which made a mournful sound as if they too felt my pain. With the lantern burning behind him, he took a couple of steps forward. I kept my eyes on him while backing away in the direction I had come. My fingers tightened around the fragment of wood I had picked up in the garden, and I primed it ready in my hand. He went back to the lantern, and, taking it down from the branch, he climbed the steps to the open door. He paused in the doorway and held the light up for me to see. I held my breath while my heart beat thunderously in my chest.

Surrounded by darkness and peculiar night-time sounds, I stood like a statue in the darkness. I struggled with my thoughts, fears, and the hopelessness of the situation I found myself in. I had two choices: him and the summer house or the outside with its thick darkness and eerie night-time sounds. Suddenly I heard the most frightful hooting sound overhead. My indecision suddenly disappeared and I bolted towards him. I ran up the steps, squeezed past him, and went inside. Whilst I felt a certain amount of relief to have left the outside expanse behind me, I had no idea of what was to come. Very gently, he took hold of my elbow, led me into a corner of the room, and pointed to an old rocking chair. I sat down in what I vaguely remembered to be Grandma's old rocking chair. The padding was now lumpy and smelt of mothballs and age, none the less, it felt familiar. I nodded my thanks without looking up at the figure that hovered above me.

I heard another chair being scraped across the wooden floor and felt his presence as he sat down directly in front of me. His sharp bony knees collided with my knees, which were tightly squeezed together. A stifled yelp escaped from my throat and I jumped up to my feet. His voice rasped suddenly and I was dragged back from the point of hysteria.

"That was an owl, Vannah," the man rasped. Explaining the sound, that very nearly had me peeing my pants. I made no reply and eyed him suspiciously. "Vannah, I may not look like the uncle you knew… …. years ago."

His calloused palms curled around my face now as he cupped my chin and moved his fingers over my cheeks. He seemed to be looking into the depths of my soul. Like burning coals in a dark cave, his eyes glowed into mine for a long time. I stiffened and clenched my teeth with a grinding sound. He loosened his grip and began cracking the joints in his fingers.

"On the outside, I know I look…" His voice tailed off. It seemed he couldn't find the words he wanted to describe himself with. I felt sorry for him, but I wanted to be absolutely certain this man was my Uncle Daniel. His voice wavered between a murmur and a whisper, and his breathing seemed deep and laboured. It was clear that he was struggling to control his emotions. "Inside I am the same person. If you care…." He paused and looked at me again. "If you would only try … try to… It wasn't supposed to be like this, Savannah. This is torture. Your indifference is killing me." He threw his hands up in dejection. I observed him but said nothing. "Just try to remember the uncle you thought was your father. It's me, Savannah. I'm your Uncle Daniel."

The pain in my heart became unbearable, and I glanced up at him briefly. His pleading eyes held mine for a moment but I looked away. Then, taking me completely by surprise, he fell to his knees and buried his head in my lap.

His body shook against mine, and the chair began to rock as if someone was pushing it back and forth. I felt all the more scared. Uncertain of his motive, I wanted to push him away from me. My body grew tight like a wound-up clock and my heart pounded. My head felt hot, and there was a throbbing in the back of my neck. I raised a hand to push him off my lap, but it remained suspended in the air. He mumbled as he sobbed and his speech became muffled by my clothing. I gripped the arms of the old rocker as I felt his tears seeping through my skirt and running down between my thighs. I had to get him off me one way or another. I looked around for the piece of wood I had picked up earlier in the garden but I couldn't see it. I closed my eyes and began to pray.

Then, as if God had heard my prayers, he got up and moved away. I cried in relief as he stood by the door. His back was turned towards me, and I began to study him. His shoulders were drooped forward like an old man; I searched my heart for memories of this figure but found none. Whilst I felt sorry for him, I could neither respond to him nor console him.

"I have tried my best, you know. I honestly tried… but I have failed you and failed my mother's memory. I have lost your inheritance. But believe me, Savannah, I tried. God knows I tried."

He walked back to me, and his long thin fingers searched for my hands. He found them tightly wrapped about my bosom. He tenderly took both my hands in his own and toyed with my fingers - the way Uncle Daniel used to do, when I was small.

He played with each of my fingers, tracing each nail as if he had found something very precious. He continued this way for sometime until my thoughts mingled with a sense of the unknown. I snatched my hands forcibly away from his grasp. My inner turmoil deepened as my thoughts carried me backwards and forwards through the years. I had yearned for an anchor to moor myself to. My grandmother had provided it. Now it would seem a light had gone out in my heart, and I had no idea how to ignite the flames of hope again. I began to rock myself back and forth in my grandmother's old chair, going over my journey from England to my arrival, hours earlier, at Peaceful View.

CHAPTER 4

We both sat staring down at the space between us. My thoughts raced as my emotions became all fired up. I sizzled with agitation - trapped in a web of emotion and intrigue. To comfort myself, I wrapped my arms around myself tightly. He reached out to me again, and I backed further into the chair. I was aware of his eyes burning through me and I detested this. He groaned and got up to his feet as if he was wondering what he should do with me. I held my breath for what seemed an eternity.

"Savannah, I suppose… I just lost interest in myself, in life. You were taken away from me… and then… Mamma died. I lost everything that meant anything to me. I know my appearance is… is making you afraid. But please don't be afraid of me. It kills me inside to see the fear in your eyes. You're the child I never had. I love you with all my heart, Savannah. I will never hurt you or do anything to harm you."

He paused, and this time I looked up at him through the tears I could no longer hold back.

"You are the reason for this tragedy." His voice was hoarse with emotion, and he breathed a sigh as if he'd put down a heavy load he had been carrying. He appeared to be blaming me for the fire and for his pathetic appearance. My throat convulsed. My head throbbed and tension mounted inside me. I no longer understand why I wanted to find him earlier. As my throat grew dryer and dryer, I wished I could swallow the many agonies I felt in my heart. I did not know if I preferred the silence or if I wanted to continue listening to this man. He had said, "I was the cause of the fire!" How could that be? What did he mean? He's crazy, disturbed, insane. I had come here to find the beautiful old colonial house had burned to the ground, and all I could do was lament its destruction.

His voice cut into my thoughts again as he rattled on, "Old Gus Stein and Robin… hold Mamma's papers. Robin was in England studying law when you left. Mamma stipulated in her will that all her papers should be given to you. Apart from money she bequeathed to us, all, everything – including me, Savannah – is left to your discretion." His speech grew laboured and he sounded drunk. With his shoulders slumped even further, he appeared no taller than me. He smiled absently and appeared to be talking to himself.

Meanwhile, I felt ensnared – locked in a small space with a crazed man who was passing himself off as my beloved Uncle Daniel. His knowledge of Grandma's affairs and the use of my pet name evoked a feeling of recognition, but this could just be coincidence. The colour of his eyes and his thin heart-shaped lips somehow looked familiar. But my heart was shrouded in doubt. I felt I was at his mercy, and all my resolve and reasoning soon deserted me. I wanted to rid myself of him.

"What is it, Savannah?" I heard him ask.

I felt my jaws tighten as I stared at him. All of a sudden, I wanted to harm him and to make him feel the pain I was feeling – the pain he had inflicted and was still inflicting upon me. I got up from the rocking chair, and though I was not conscious my lips were forming words, I could hear my own voice swell and fill the room. I reached into my soul and found the strength that had deserted me.

"I'm not sure," I heard myself answering him. "I think I'm in shock. This is all too much. I've heard enough, had enough. I can't take this charade anymore."

My voice seemed to come from a remote place deep inside me – a place burning with a desire to hurt him. With a fixed and malicious look on my face, I bolted towards him. I struck him with the clump of wood I had picked up in the garden. I had no idea how it had found its way back into my hand, but I was raining blows on him with it. I kicked, clawed, and scratched him; then I pounded my fists into him. Like a deranged woman I, attacked him with every fibre of strength I could muster. He braced himself against the wall, and I pounded my fists into his bony back. I felt a sharp pain in my wrists, but the sensation only gave more passion to the force I exerted upon him. He turned around to face me and to hold me off, and I dug my long nails down one side of his face. To finish off, I aimed a kick into his crotch. He dropped to the floor, rolled himself into a ball, and covered his head with one hand; the other hand was clamped between his thighs.

I spat at him and screamed, "Do you have any idea what you've done, you idiot, you half-crazed fool? Do you? It would have been better for you if you had thrown yourself on the fire and burnt with the house. I will see to it you rot in hell for the rest of your miserable life. I will make you pay for this, if it's the last thing I do." Then I demanded, "Who are you? Tell me, you impostor. Who are you?"

I walked away from him to the far corner of the room. Exhausted, I ran one hand over my face to wipe away the tears running down my cheeks. The smell of fresh blood infiltrated my nostrils. I looked down at my hands. Shocked at what I saw there, I looked over at him. He was crouched in a heap in the spot he had fallen, and there was blood dripping from his face on to the floor. I was dazed by the sight, and the ferocity of my attack dawned on me. He had done nothing to defend himself, except to hit the floor and roll his body into a ball. What if he really was Uncle Daniel?

My chest began to tighten, and my breathing became shallower with each breath. I felt an asthma attack coming on. I threw myself down in the rocking chair and wedged my head between my knees. He dashed to my side and placed one hand on my back and the other between my breasts. A voice from another time echoed in my head as he counted and repeated the routine Grandma had taught me, and which, Uncle Daniel had done with me many times when I was small. He pulled my shoulders upright and encouraged me to relax my breathing until the worst passed. This wretched-looking creature had to be my beloved Uncle Daniel, I thought. He sat me back into the chair and rocked me gently. I closed my eyes in utter shame.

In time, I put up my hand to signal to him the attack had passed. He held on to my hand. This time I did not snatch it away from him; instead, I squeezed his hand tightly. He reciprocated by doing the same. I kept my eyes closed and rocked back and forth using the muscles in my back. I heard him moving around, and heard the sound of water being poured. A match was struck and a flame was lit. I knew he was in pain and knew too, I had hurt him. How was I going to explain my actions to him, and how was I ever going to make it up to him?

"May I have a drink please, Uncle Daniel? I am thirsty."

He came and stooped down in front of me. I opened my eyes, and, for a while, we studied each other's face. He felt my forehead and then ran the back of his hand over my cheek.

"My little girl! My little Princess Savannah! You have finally come home. I have waited so long for this day. I have never stopped missing you and your mischief. Apart from…" I knew only too well the words he couldn't bring himself to say. I thought I would talk to him about it later when I felt stronger and we were used to each other again. "Everyone believed Mamma's heart broke in two the day you left. Nothing was the same without you. Even Dick moped!"

"Ooooh! Please don't… please. Enough for one day. I can't bear anymore," I whimpered into my hands, feeling guilty and ashamed of what I had done to him.

Tears hovered on the surface of my eyes; I was sorry I couldn't take it all back. I put my hand over his mouth to stop him talking. The devoted look in his now swollen eyes together with the awful scratches down one side of his face was torture enough. How his pitifully thin body took the blows I rained on him, I will never know. If I could step back into time, I'd have gone back to England instantly. I didn't want to hear the mention of my grandmother or of my friend Dick. It was all much too much. The last few hours had seen me at my lowest ebb since the day the telegram arrived with the news of Grandma's death. Finally the floodgates opened, and I gave way to tears. I broke down, and, burying my face into my uncle's shoulder, I wept.

CHAPTER 5

My weeping finally ceased. Uncle Daniel tenderly dried my face and fetched a bowl of water to soothe my face. Next he placed a steaming mug of Grandma's notorious green tea into my hand. I didn't have an ounce of strength to protest.

"Drink this, Savannah. It's good for you," he said.

As a child, I had hated this tea. Grandma used to force me to drink it, claiming it had healing powers. Uncle Daniel now went off to change his blood-and-tear-stained shirt while I drank the tea. Surprisingly, I found I quite enjoyed it. I took two giant puffs from my asthma pump to relieve the tightness I still felt in my chest.

"That should do it for another year," I said, putting the pump back into my handbag.

Uncle Daniel returned with a table-top fan, which he placed next to me.

"I'll put this on for you. I can see you are hot."

I smiled at him as the fan began to hum on a small round table in the corner by the rocking chair. I glanced at him sitting beside me and cringed when my eyes rested on his face. Consumed with a sense of guilt, shame, and loss, I began to feel cold. I shivered, and Uncle Daniel dashed off to fetch me a blanket. He placed the blanket around me and I hugged it close. It provided me with much-needed warmth, but nothing could compensate for the turmoil inside. Silence fell between us again, but this time, I felt no discomfort. It was more a feeling of resignation. We sat inches away from each other, each of us fighting our own ghosts from the past – a past neither one of us could relive or re-create anymore. The present waited as still as the silence between us.

My body soon began to feel weary, and my eyes struggled to remain open. Feelings of limpness drifted down my arms and legs, and the fear and anxiety vanished. Rain started to pitter-patter on the rooftop and soon became a full-scale downpour. Huge drops of water beat down on the roof, bounced off onto the windows, and tumbled down the sides of the summer house. I could smell the sweet scent of the rain as it quenched the parched earth. The words in Uncle Daniel's last letter to me before I left England for the island came back like a dream: "Savannah, we've had a drought here for the last six months. It's very dry here now."

As the air began to cool, the temperature dropped rapidly inside the Summerhouse, and my body chilled further. Sweet long-forgotten memories and sensations crawled all over my mind, carrying my thoughts along with each drop of rain. A semi-conscious feeling of rain-induced sleep soothed my fraught nerves. My head lolled, and my eyelids grew heavy. The mug slipped through my fingers and met the floor with a thud. My jaws moved as I mumbled but did not know what I said. I had the sensation I was walking, but my feet did not seem to be touching the cool wooden floor. My head was being cushioned now, very gently, amidst soft smell of lavender, and my body curled into the feathery softness of a bed.

I was vaguely aware of Grandma. Her scent filled my nostrils, and her hand stroked me to sleep. She moved like a shadow around the room and spoke in a far-away voice about a mosquito net. Something spread itself all around me, draping the little daybed like a shroud. I protested and tried to sit up but was pushed gently back against the softness of feather pillows. Grandma's voice echoed through my head, and I felt a smile settling over my face. Tender strokes floated through my hair and took my fears away.

A voice whispered into my ear, "Why fight the inevitable, princess? It's futile and exhausting. Have a peaceful night's sleep. God bless."

The words blended with the sounds of raindrops, soft wind, and rumbling thunder. Flashes of lightning lit up the room, and I felt a deep sense of peace. Beautiful images and laughing voices floated through my mind- and tranquillity beckoned to me.

My head grew heavier, and I sank deeper into the softness of the pillows. As the soothing sounds of raindrops caressed me, I gave up fighting, and my limbs succumbed to nature's very own sleeping pill.

CHAPTER 6

Savannah Meet Bobby

I sat by the window, savouring the sweet smells of the clean rain-washed earth and watching the clouds over the mountaintops. In the distance, thunder roared like a pride of angry lions, and flashes of lightning cut zigzag paths through the grey sky. I shuddered, for the heavens seemed to be brooding in sympathy at my loss – the loss of a beautiful old house that had stood here for generations between these clusters of hills. A sense of profound loneliness surrounded my heart now, and I walked away from the window. I sat down on the bed, fearing I was going to cry again. I'd done enough of that last night; another weeping fit, and I was sure I would drown myself in my own tears. I dabbed at my eyes and looked around me. I noticed an envelope with my name on it on Grandma's old dresser. I picked it up, unfolded the sheet of paper inside, and began to read.

"Dearest Savannah, you will not find me here when you wake up, for I have gone into town. Bobby will take care of you until I return. He is there with you in the summer house. I have gone to the barbers. From there, I intend to pick up some groceries, see Gus Stein, and hopefully catch up with Robin too. Ken came by this morning, but you were peacefully asleep. I didn't want to wake you up. He brought your luggage. They are in your Aunt Eva's house. Ken will be coming back later this evening to see you. I am getting Eva's house ready for us. It's going to be home now. Savannah, I want you to know how happy I am to have you home. I know it has been very hard for you to understand what has gone on over the years. We will talk, for I hope you are going to be here for a long time. Seeing you again is a joy. I am so ecstatic. Although you gave me a battering last night, I am still overjoyed to have you home. I know we are going to get on famously! It will be like the old days, I'm sure. Back soon. Yours, Uncle Daniel."

My uncle's words left me weak. I could do nothing besides fold the sheet of paper and replace it back in the envelope. Not quite knowing what to do with myself now, I went back to sit by the window where I had been sitting since I woke. Once more, I peered out into the bleakness that had replaced my dreams.

Now, except for straggling rose bushes and trees that had grown out of control, I saw no flowers to gladden my broken heart or quench my famished eyes. Tucked away beneath a mass of trees, a cornucopia of flowers had once draped rainbow colours over the shingled domed roof of the summer house. I sat thinking about the words in Uncle Daniel's note. A terrible guilt and sense of doubt hugged me like a second skin. I had planned to spend six months with him on the island; now I wasn't sure about anything. I looked down at the envelope in my hand and suddenly remembered Bobby. Uncle Daniel's note said that he was there with me. If ever I needed someone or a remedy for all my woes, it was my cousin Bobby. I got to my feet, wondering what Bobby was doing on the island and why Uncle Daniel had not mentioned he was there. Then I pushed away my questioning thoughts and smiled to myself. I thought of the scrapes I used to get into with Bobby, our protectiveness of each other, and the many secrets we had sworn to keep until the day we died!

"What a lovely surprise. The best piece of news I've had so far," I said to myself.

I placed the envelope with Uncle Daniel's note on the dresser and walked out into the main room, but no one was there. I noticed a kettle on a portable gas stove in a corner. I checked it had water and then lit the ring under the kettle. I went to the door leading to the gardens outside. Just as I opened the door, a man jumped up brandishing a machete sharpened on both sides! Frantically, I slammed the door shut and slid the security bolt into place. I found the key for the lock hanging from a cord, thrust it into the door, and locked it. I saw a length of steel pipe leaned up in the corner by the door. I picked it up and braced myself.

"Gee, Savannah. It's me, Bobby. I didn't mean to scare you," the machete-wielding thug said from the other side of the door.

I yelled back at him from my side, "You long-haired lout. I don't believe you. Prove to me you are who you say you are and don't kid yourself. I'm no pushover."

Like most females I could be erratic at times. But underneath, I was not only a woman of colour but one of strength and resilience. No long-haired, machete-wielding bully was going to make me pee in my pants.

"What can I say to convince you, Savannah? OK… I can tell you your birthday. How's that?"

I could tell he was standing on top of the steps and could almost feel his body heat through the door. Shifting my weight on to my back leg, I positioned myself for attack. If I had to use the steel pipe, I would aim to inflict maximum damage. I intended to make sure he wasn't going to get away intact.

"It's a start. Go on," I said, taking aim. I was ready to hit him on the head should the door came crashing in.

I'd had enough of fires and scary morons. No one was going to terrify me again.

"You were born in the month of September. Your birthday's two days before mine. How's that?"

It was going to take a whole lot more than that to persuade me. This was just one nightmare too many. I pushed for further proof.

"I'm not convinced. Tell me something from my childhood only Bobby knew."

He laughed out aloud, then drawled in his American accent.

"OK, I'll give you a choice. I can tell you about the night of Aunt Rhonda's wake or the day three acres of corn went up in smoke!"

"Oh crumbs!" I said from behind the door.

No other living person knew I was the one who had set fire to the cornfield. This had to be none other than my cousin Bobby. Who else would have awakened this memory? Moreover, there were four of us in the room on the night of Aunt Rhonda's wake, but no other person knew about the cornfield fire. I still wasn't fully convinced. I wasn't going to be fooled, and neither was I going to fall so easily. I pressed him further.

"It will take more than that... to persuade me. You'll have to do better than that," I said.

"Alright, Savannah, there's a scar on your right calf – about nine inches down from your knee."

I looked down at my leg. Though the scar he described had faded over the years and was now covered by a small tattoo, the memory of how it happened had refused to fade with the passage of time. However, it was one more memory I didn't care to recall. So far the machete brute had awakened two of the nightmares I had battled to keep buried in my heart. I said nothing.

"Will you be convinced... if I tell you how you got the scar, Savannah?"

I flung the door open, stood in the doorway, and brandished the length of steel pipe aloft.

"Move a muscle, and I'll send your head into orbit!"

It dawned on me I was fast becoming a warrior in my own right – and it wasn't a moment too soon.

Bobby screwed up his face and slid his tongue to one corner of his mouth. I laughed, remembering the way we used to greet each other if one or the other was feeling sad. Bobby's vivid hazel eyes lit up as he stood on the steps stroking his cute little beard. I made a face at him and then began mocking him.

"I see nothing has changed. You're still the bushman you always were," I said, rolling my eyes.

I did not want to show how terrified I had been moments earlier. Bobby's mood switched suddenly, and he glanced around like a nervous animal! His eyes seemed to be probing the hills around Peaceful View. I pretended I hadn't noticed this and tried to make light of things.

"Well, Bob, aren't you going to say something? Greet me? Hug me? Then again… you might be planning to chop me up with your machete?" I said, remembering how as a boy he would not be parted from his first machete.

Bobby relaxed a little and rewarded me with a dazzling white smile. His apparent bashfulness, or whatever it was, amused me; as a boy, Bobby had had no fear. He was never shy and was a monster that cheated at everything. He never played games fairly and always had to be the winner. He would put worms, toads, and frogs into my dungaree pockets, down my back, or in my school satchel. Maybe it wasn't too late to get my own back on him, I wickedly thought to myself!

"OK Bob, if you won't talk to me, at least come and have a cup of tea with me."

I winked mischievously at him, and that seemed to do the trick. Bobby shoved the handle of the monstrous machete under one arm, took off his shoes, and followed me inside. He immediately locked and bolted the door behind us! I looked at the door, a little anxious at this decisive action.

"Bob… why did you do that? I mean…lock and bolt the door?" I asked, walking towards the stove where the kettle whistled furiously.

"You can't be too careful, Savannah. Know what I mean?" He stood at my side. "I'll make the coffee. You sit down."

He pulled Grandma's old rocker towards me. I sat down to await my first hot drink of the day. I watched as Bobby moved around what used to be Grandma's sitting room. Here she wrote letters, listened to music on her ancient gramophone, read her many carefully-preserved old books, or just hid away from us all. I wondered what Grandma would make of a gas stove in her sitting room, not to mention, its now shabby state. Bobby looked over his shoulder at me and flashed another of his super-white smiles. He seemed pleased to see me but was tense. In no time, though, two mugs of coffee and a plateful of tea cakes were placed on the little round table. He sat down, and we picked up our mugs simultaneously.

Bobby had changed considerably. His skin looked baby soft, smooth, with not a trace of a laughter line. He wasn't as tall as I'd imagined him to be, but none the less, my heart swelled with pride as

I drank in the handsome features of my long-lost cousin. He was truly good-looking. He had fine features and pearly white teeth. His neat little beard and long curling eyelashes added the final alluring virtues to his face. He was handsome in a slightly rugged yet delicate way. It had been over twenty-one years since we had last seen each other, and I was eager for Bobby to fill me in on the missing years. I found it hard to contain myself and began to question him.

"How has your life been, Bob? Are you married? Do you have any children? What have you been doing with yourself? I am so surprised to find you here. I honestly thought you were still in the US. Uncle Daniel never told me you were here. I want to hear every last detail," I said breathlessly.

I rested my elbows on the table and cradled my face in my hands as my mind went back in time. Bobby had left the island two days after I had. He had travelled with six other cousins. They all went to join their parents in the United States. Six more went to Canada to join their parents, and I went to England with my sister Melody, and cousins, Tamara, Jennifer, Hazel, Dinah, and Joy. It was a period Grandma had called "an exodus of her family".

Grandma had arranged the dates of our travel as close together as possible. She had said, "If we all went together, it would be easier for her to accept."

We had bid each other goodbye and had tearfully clung to Grandma. We promised to write and never to lose touch with each other. We planned to return to the island at least once a year for a family get together. However, our plans were never realised, for Grandma died, and our family, as we knew it, disintegrated. Foreign shores became the adopted homes for mostly all of Grandma's children and grandchildren. I felt sadness creeping in again as yesterday's events came back to my mind.

"Savannah… are you listening to me at all?" Bobby drawled and lent over to touch the side of my face with the back of his index finger.

"Oh, I'm so sorry, Bob. I -I was far away in thought. I'm all ears now. Do go on."

I pulled myself back from the past and looked intently into Bobby's gorgeous face.

"I'll start again. You ready?"

I nodded enthusiastically.

"I lived in the US, as you know… and yes, I had a good life there going to school, then on to college, and, finally, university. I studied agriculture like Uncle Daniel. I go back to the States for a month every so often." He grinned from time to time as he went on. "After I gained my degree, I worked for a company doing research stuff. I won't bore you with agricultural talk, though."

He threw a dismissive hand up in the air and pulled out a pack of cigarettes with the other. He offered me one.

"No thanks. Keep talking," I urged him on.

My cousin's company was just what I needed to take my mind off things. I sat engrossed as I listened and visualised us as children. The Bobby I knew twenty-one or so years ago and the Bobby sitting with me now couldn't be more different. I became impatient to catch up.

"Anyhow, my heart was always here. When Grandma suffered the last stroke, I simply had to come home. I vowed then I would be back within a year or two. I have been here five years now."

He grinned again, tossing his shoulder-length hair backwards. The little summer house soon rang with laughter as we giggled like mischievous seven-year-olds again.

"You're not married then?" I asked teasingly.

I would have heard the news, even if it were after the event, as it often happened. With family scattered around the world, this was frequently the case.

"Once or twice I came close. I'm not ready for that shit yet. It's serious stuff, and life's for living. I want to live. Look, Savannah, girls are great. But they are just too… needy. Any wife of mine should have spirit and independence. But above all, she has to be educated, with a career of her own. I don't want a woman who cuts and pastes bits of other people's lives or views and makes it into her life. I want a woman with confidence, with views of her own – not a weak one who's entirely dependent on me. She will have to shine like a bright star! I haven't found her yet. No children either."

Bobby eased back into the chair, looking far more relaxed now. I wasn't keen on the slang words he reverted to from time to time but decided to excuse him. Perhaps later we could pick up on them again. He'd referred to marriage as "shit"! It shocked me, and Grandma must have turned in her grave too. Nevertheless, I was relishing every precious moment spent with my cousin.

"I want to be around for my children – unlike our parents. I know they went abroad to seek a better life for us. But in truth, I never understood why they left in the first place. I had a great childhood with our grandparents. But having my own parents around…" Bobby stood up, and I calculated he must be roughly five feet eight inches tall. I sensed resentment in his tone and wondered what pains he harboured around his early life without his parents. I guess, if I am honest, I had hang-ups and anger too. I just never confronted them. "Besides… I need my space. So here I am having a cup of coffee with my favourite cousin."

He sat down again, folded his arms, crossed his legs, and looked enquiringly at me.

"Your turn, Savannah. Tell me everything about you:"

I heard Bobby's words but didn't answer him straight away. I was choked up inside. I, too, had wanted to return home to pay my last respects to a Grandma I loved dearly, but my father refused to pay my air fair. I was still at school then, and there was no way I could have paid for myself. I had sworn never to forgive my father for what I saw as a mean and cruel act. But then, there were so many unresolved issues between my father and me. In the end, I had to get away from his disturbing behaviour and his prison-like house. The moment I was able to, I was gone. Five months before my eighteenth birthday; I packed my suitcases and left. I had been born a survivor, and the strength and resilience I often mustered left me breathless. Hardly eighteen and not quite a woman, I entered a daunting world to fend for myself. I could feel my expression changing as grief combined with memories and resentment.

"Savannah, what's up? Did I say something wrong?" Bobby asked, looking concerned.

I shook my head and walked to one of the windows. I felt hot and clammy and needed to feel and smell the outside air.

"No, Bobby… it's me. I get all screwed up inside when Grandma is mentioned. I can't talk about her for very long. I mean… I don't like to. Memories of her are locked away in my heart. It hurt to talk about her. Oh, Bobby… why can't I just get over her death like everyone else? I miss her so. I have never stopped missing her. I don't think I'll ever get used to the idea she is dead. Do you know….when I woke up this morning, I expected her to walk in at any moment? Coming back here has been… hard. I smell her, see her, and hear her. She fills my head and…"

I swallowed the rest of what I couldn't and didn't want to say. I had resolutely promised myself I wasn't going to cry again; now I simply couldn't guarantee I wouldn't. Bobby pulled his chair closer to sit next to me as I flopped down into the rocking chair. We wrapped our arms around each other and began to hum a little tune Grandma used to sing to us when we were small.

A Song Grandma Sang at Bedtime

"Sleep and rest. Sleep and rest… rest - rest on Grandma's breast. Mamma will come to thee sooon. Mamma will come to her babe in the nest – silver sails coming out of the west. Under a golden moooon, while my little one, while my pretty one, sleep."

"We sang that together without even thinking about it," I said, looking around and feeling lost in a sea of turbulent emotions and thoughts.

"I don't know what it is about that little tune. But if ever I feel afraid or worried about anything or when I'm feeling lonesome, I sing it. It makes me feel a whole lot better every time," Bobby commented reflectively as he stroked my hand and ruffled my sleep-tousled hair.

This soft side of Bobby was far removed from the Bobby I knew as a child. I'd never imagined him as having a soft centre. He'd grown into a sweet, caring man and was as sentimental as I was. Grandma would have been so proud of him.

"Do you know, Bobby, I sing it for exactly the same reasons too? I will sing it to my children one day. What about you, Bobby? Do you think you will sing it to your children?" I asked, hoping this wonderful and tuneful little song would never die.

It was a sure-fire sleeping pill when we were children. Grandma's pretty voice would sing us all into our individual world of dreams.

"I am sure we both will, Savannah. Now, how about another coffee?" Bobby got to his feet, and his nervous energy returned again.

"Yes, please… but can I have tea instead? I usually don't drink coffee. We can sit outside on the steps. It will be nice to breathe some fresh air and gaze at the hills again."

I went into the inner room to fetch my handbag and gather my thoughts. I sat down on the daybed to clear my head and register the fact that I was actually sitting talking to Bobby and that I was at Peaceful View again. I wondered whether I was the cause of Bobby's nervousness but couldn't see why. Perhaps a day or two would change all that as we picked up where we had left off.

"Savannah... you alright in there?" Bobby called from the other side of the door.

"Yes, I'm all right. I'll be right there."

I picked up my bag, eager now to get outside even though it was wet and overcast. The summer house suddenly seemed like a prison. While I waited for Bobby, I began to wander around, touching and stroking objects from my childhood. I hadn't had a chance to see the old place in daylight yet. I pulled back a corner of the curtains and peered out across the gardens.

The air was heavy with moisture from the previous night's rain. Life on Peaceful View looked sorry for itself. Every bit of vegetation I saw, hung limp as if in sad meditation. I began to wonder whether it was time to let go and to bury the memories that had me chained so firmly to the past. Just then, Bobby appeared behind me. Draping his arm around my shoulders, he led me back to Grandma's rocking chair.

"Savannah, we all miss the old girl. Look at Uncle D. He has never accepted grandma's death. If I hadn't come home when I did, you'd have seen his name in the cemetery too. He's a broken man, Savannah. Go easy on him, I beg you. He needs you, Savannah –he needs us both. You shook him up pretty badly last night. But he understands. We both do."

As he spoke, his gaze came to rest on a family photograph on the wall. I had glanced at the same photograph last night but couldn't bear to study the features of those I had loved and lost. I found the whole idea of death disconcerting. My feelings were still very raw, and for years, I had struggled to come to terms with my loss. Grandma and my Aunt Vicky had been the mother figures in my early life. My heart ached to think they were not there anymore. Nothing or no one could replace them. My mood danced now, on either side of a delicate strand—as memories I had keep close to my heart, begin to surface.

I sat passively beside Bobby. My head hung low as my thoughts turned inward again. Last night I had rained a volley of blows upon

Uncle Daniel. I knew I had a temper but had no idea I was capable of such violence. I'd beaten the only person I had left who loved me unconditionally.

"Savannah…" Bobby called and touched my hand affectionately. I looked absently at him. He appeared to be feasting on his fingernails and spoke through his biting. "Look, Savannah, there's something I have to tell you."

"What is it, Bobby? What's troubling you?"

"Savannah, promise me you'll not say a word. You can't tell anyone what I'm about to tell you, especially not Uncle Daniel."

The light in Bobby's hazel eyes grew dim, and a troubled look settled over his face. I had no idea what to expect, so I waited patiently.

"You have my word, Bobby," I said, using my eyes to do the pleading for me.

"Savannah…" he called again, and a long pause followed.

He appeared to be wondering whether or not to reveal to me what was on his mind. I sighed for I was getting rather uptight at yet another mystery tour I wasn't prepared for.

"Savannah, what do you remember about our Uncle Claude?"

The question surprised me. This was the second time in a short while that Bobby had made a reference to Claude; the uncle I pretended had died years ago. In my mind he did not exist; I had buried all memory of that evil beast. Now, Bobby was about to compel me to talk about something I'd rather leave buried. It seemed a choice had been made for me. My face hardened, my jaws tightened, and my teeth came together in a crunch. Claude's hateful countenance appeared in my mind. I felt I had been exposed, undone! I began to pace the floor while Claude seemed to stare at me with venom in his eyes.

CHAPTER 7

Claude

I felt I had been forced to respond to Bobby's question, and I wondered where it would end. I decided to begin with the least painful memories and then feel my way along and see what happened.

"I remember he hated me. I never knew why. I remember too that whenever he got a chance, he'd hurt me physically. A pinch here, a flying kick there, a burn, or…" I shrugged, as I tried to hide from a time in my past, which always waited to trip me up. "Grandma and Uncle Daniel never let me out of their sight whenever he was around. There was something…" I kept pacing the floor until I found myself standing in front of Grandma's old writing desk. I had been sitting down for hours, and, frankly, my bottom had grown numb. But I eased my body up to sit on top of the desk none the less.

"The fire..." said Bobby, as he strolled over to tilt my chin up so I looked directly into his eyes. "It was Claude. Claude set the house on fire. Look, Savannah, he has threatened the day you return to claim your inheritance...."

I heard no more. My heart began to race as I became preoccupied with my thoughts. I wondered how many times in twenty-four hours was I to feel so utterly out of my depth. Yet everything was making sense and falling into place like missing pieces from a jigsaw puzzle. The only trouble was that this was no ordinary puzzle. I realised, too, that what I had mistaken for eccentricity in Uncle Daniel was more likely the years of abuse at Claude's hand. In addition, I realised I had seen fear in Uncle Daniel's eyes but had mistaken it for cowardice. Uncle Daniel's measured words last night had given me the feeling that he was holding something back from me. But I'd sensed this for months. This was my reason for not wanting him to know I was coming home.

Over the last six months, Uncle Daniel's letters had become cagey. He had ceased his jovial banter about his struggles to keep the farm afloat, and his letters got shorter and shorter. Now it was all making sense. But why on earth would Claude want me dead? Sure he hated and abused me as a child. But I was no longer a child and was no threat to him whatsoever. Either I was missing something or Bobby was trying to scare me. I decided to keep my fears to myself.

"Uncle D..." Bobby seemed to be looking straight through me now,"... he wants Mr Stein and Robin present when he talks to you. They are going to hand Grandma's papers to you. As you know, Grandma's will states you are to have her papers... with the title deed for Peaceful View. I gave Uncle D my word that I wouldn't say anything to you until then. Keep this conversation between us quiet, please. It never took place... OK?"

Bobby sat next to me on top of Grandma's desk as I listened to his gut-churning revelations. My suspense grew as Bobby continued.

"Look, Savannah, you have to prepare yourself. The ride's going to get rough!"

I exhaled a long slow breath, which I had been holding on to for a long time. A little voice in my head told me to conceal my thoughts.

"Don't worry. I won't breathe a word."

I reached across and touched Bobby's little beard to reassure him. But I felt a cold emptiness in my stomach.

Why

"You deserve to know the truth, Savannah," Bobby said, walking over to the kettle. He flicked his lighter, and a circle of blue flames spread under the kettle. I watched the flames for a time, not knowing what to say.

"Savannah, Claude is obsessed. The threat is serious. It's real."

"Wow," I said, finally clasping my hands together and stretching them out in front of me. "What have I done? What did I do to him, Bobby? Do you have any idea why he hates me so?"

"Grandma's love and now the will. He resents it – resents you. Grandma leaves you everything…"

Bobby's words smacked of unfairness, and what he said simply wasn't true.

"What do you mean? Grandma didn't leave me everything. Uncle Daniel's welfare is left to me. He and I are joint inheritors. The place is left to my discretion. It belongs to us all, along with money left to everyone. Do you think if I could trade this place to have my loved ones back, I wouldn't? Money cannot buy what matters." Bobby tossed his long hair away from his face. He looked preoccupied, as if carrying the world on his shoulders, or maybe he was angry at my outburst. I suspected that he, too, in spite of his revelations, was holding something back from me. I decided to test the waters. "Do you resent Grandma's will too, Bobby?" I asked, fixing my gaze straight at him.

"No, Savannah, I don't. Uncle D and I believe Grandma's done the right thing. The old girl knew you'd follow her directions. Grandma knew you would be fair to us all."

Bobby defined the word "fair" with a distinct tone in his voice.

"I should be offended you even think to ask me that. But I guess I'd do the same if I was in your position."

Then under his breath he whispered softly as if speaking to himself.

"I'm not in your position, though, am I, Savannah?"

I looked away from my cousin, for my feelings about him had changed in an instant. Bobby's words and tone disturbed me, but what I couldn't put a finger on was the resentment I detected in his tone.

"This whole will thing has turned into an oppressive nightmare," I said, sliding down from the desk. If I was going to find out Bobby's true colours, I'd have to stay cool and humour him into a false sense of security. "Thank you, Bobby," I said. Then I added, "Who knows… I may not get another chance to thank you. Since I arrived here, it has been hell. I was welcomed with an inferno. Then, as if that weren't bad enough, Uncle Daniel scared me half to death. Now I have another moron of an uncle, who wants to kill me. What a welcome home, eh?"

I dragged myself back to Grandma's old rocking chair and sat down again. The chair was about the only thing I felt sure about. I was no longer sure how I ought to feel. It appeared I was swimming against the tide without a hope of rescue. Bobby lit another cigarette, inhaled, and blew a miasma of smoke into the room. I watched the greyish white smoke morph, disturbingly, into nooses. At least three drifted close and circled above my head. I felt relieved I wasn't a superstitious soul, or I'd see this as some sort of forewarning signalling - impending doom. I swiped at them, and they dispersed and drifted away. I finally found a logical question to ask.

"Bob... did anyone actually see that scoundrel set fire to the house?"

"Yes," he replied, watching me. Then, all of a sudden, Bobby kicked the leg of the rocking chair I was seated in. He then thumped the table top upsetting the mugs and, of all things, angrily kicked my handbag across the room. I jumped up, whacked him around the head, and, with a forceful push, sent him staggering across the room.

"What do you think you are doing? Pick up my bag right now... cheek!"

I glared at him with fire in my eyes. Taking his frustrations out on the table and chair was one thing; kicking my handbag across the room was quite another. I believed I was the real target of Bobby's frustrations and certainly wasn't pleased. After all, I should be the one showing feelings of frustration!

"Savannah, you pack one hell of a punch for someone so small. I meant nothing. It was just something to..." He held up his hands above his head in mock surrender. "I saw him but got there too late... too late to save the house!" Then, out of the blue, he began to rant. "There's two hundred acres of land here. Claude could have his pick of any section of land he wanted to build his own house on. I'm sure you have no intention of denying any of us our right. I don't understand it. Don't understand why he did it."

Why

While I agreed with Bobby's declaration, I had an uncanny feeling the statement was a double-edged sword – like his monstrous machete. Bobby had read my intentions correctly, but he could never understand I would gladly give it all away to have my loved ones back. I was convinced there and then that Bobby was involved with Claude.

"He has forfeited any right now. I'm just glad Uncle Daniel wasn't involved," I said. The words had scarcely left my lips when we heard footsteps outside! These were followed by three quick tapping sounds on the door. Bobby grabbed his machete and sprinted to the window. I sat rigid in Grandma's old rocker looking at the door and waiting for the moment it would come crashing in.

"Shhhhh..." Bobby said, finger pressed against his lips.

"Who is it?" I whispered.

"Shhhhh... quiet," Bobby hissed like a snake in my direction.

"Don't even breathe, Savannah. Go into the back room, lock the door, and stay there until I come to get you."

I got up from the chair and tiptoed my way into the back room. I closed the door behind me and sat shell-shocked on the daybed. I felt trapped in a nightmare. I had to get to a place of safety.

The sounds of jingling keys outside nearly made me jump out of my skin. I sat bolt upright listening. There was a knock on the door behind me. I breathed easy as I realised Uncle Daniel had returned.

"How is my little tiger princess?" Uncle Daniel's question was followed by whispering, but I couldn't make out what was being said. "Savannah, I'm back," he said as I cautiously opened the door. "There you are. You must have had a good rest. You look as fresh as the morning dew. Come,"

I groaned at Uncle Daniel's comment, for he had no idea of the pain in my heart. He stepped into the room and planted a kiss on my brow. Then, taking me by the hand, he led me back into the outer room. I immediately went to sit in Grandma's rocker, and, as I rocked myself back and forth, my thoughts raced through every known possible means of escape.

I glanced regretfully at Uncle Daniel whom I had attacked, as though driven by the devil. He had a black eye, his face and upper lip were swollen, and one side of his face dropped awkwardly. Then there were those awful scratches down one cheek. All in all, I had managed to transform his face. As if my poor uncle hadn't already been horsewhipped by life's unkindness - I had waded straight in, and whipped him some more. I was pleased to see he had taken an interest in himself, but I suspected he had done so for me and not for himself. He'd had a haircut and was clean-shaven now. Gone were those awful tangles, hanging from his head and face. I looked away quickly and purposely focused my eyes on Bobby, who was busy packing groceries and other bits and pieces into boxes. Aunt Eva's house was going to be my next prison until I could plan my escape.

My mind alternated between the loss of the birth home I loved, my cruel assault on my uncle, and the memories that bound me so persistently to the past. Bobby's revelations, however, troubled me the most. It appeared there was never going to be an end to the terrors I had innocently walked into. I looked down at my clothes and realised I was still wearing the clothes I had arrived in yesterday. How I longed for the unpredictable weather and the safe solitude of my flat back in England.

"I need a bath," I said to no one in particular.

"The shower still works, in spite of its age, Savannah. Bobby repaired it only a week ago. He is very handy. He can fix anything. Isn't that so, Bob?" Uncle Daniel looked fondly at his nephew. "Why didn't you use it, Savannah? Did you forget the summer house had a shower?" Uncle Daniel asked with a lopsided wink.

"I guess I must have," I replied.

"When we've finished packing up here, Savannah, we are going down to Eva's. The house is ready for us now. Bobby painted it a month or so ago. He'd had this premonition. What did you say at the time, Bob?"

Bobby thought for a while, then, looking over at me, he pressed a finger to his lips. I winked and he gave me the thumb's up. I took the sign as an affirmation of my promise and smiled wearily.

"I'd said I had a feeling we were going to have unexpected visitors."

"And the rest? You're hiding your light under a bushel, Bobby," said Uncle Daniel.

"I'd said family members were going to be coming home this Christmas."

"That's right. Imagine that, Savannah. That's you… my princess. You've come home."

Uncle Daniel looked over at me sitting in Grandma's rocking chair. I hoped I'd not given away what I knew or what I was feeling in my heart.

"I wasn't far wrong, was I? Let's just say… I have inherited Grandma's talent," Bobby said, looking proud of himself. He looked from me to Uncle Daniel; then in the same breath he said, "OK guys, it's time to go. The ugly one's pad will be home for us now."

Any other time, I would have laughed at Bobby's description of our dear ugly Aunt Eva. But I had nothing to laugh about, and, somehow, his quip seemed to have passed Uncle Daniel by too. Bobby picked up the largest of the three boxes and nodded his head to get me to follow him. I put on my shoes and went to stand by the door. I was desperate now to escape the confines of what had become two claustrophobic rooms. I'd have a well-deserved shower once I got to Aunt Eva's house. Maybe that will ease my troubled thoughts and send me to sleep. I may just wake to find the last twenty-four hours was all one horrible dream.

"Mamma used to say things were about to happen… and then those things did happen."

Uncle Daniel reflected on Bobby's earlier comment about his having inherited Grandma's talent. Bobby traded glances with me, then quickly interrupted Uncle Daniel's thoughts about his mother.

"Uncle D, it's time to go. Savannah must be hungry. We'll come back and pick up the rest and lock up here."

Uncle Daniel swallowed down the last drop of coffee from his mug and picked up another of the boxes. Bobby was first out the door, his machete resting on top of the box he carried. It dawned on me Uncle Daniel suspected or had evidence that Claude was hiding somewhere on the property. The place was so vast. Claude could be anywhere, and no one would suspect he was watching their every move. I followed behind Bobby with Uncle Daniel close on my heels; one of his hands rested firmly on my shoulder.

CHAPTER 8

On Route to Aunt Eva's House

    The journey to Aunt Eva's house was about a quarter of a mile. It took us through the gardens leading from the summer house then onto a path that was unfamiliar to me. This new path branched off around the back of the cemetery and joined the old path some distance into the meadow. The path I remembered led from the family home, past the foot of the twin hills and the cemetery, through the maze of fruit trees, and into the field where the men in the family used to play cricket after dinner in the evenings. There had been seesaws, swings, and various playhouses for us children to dash in an out of. I used to wander down the old path at all hours of the day and night. One evening I had seen the hideous figure of a man squatting on top of a rock in the twin hills. I wondered what had become of the old path. Everything looked different to me now that I was an adult, but my mind wanted to follow the route my memory clung to. Feeling lost, I soon thought back to a couple of months previously – another point in my life when the plans I had for the future had seemed to hang in jeopardy.

Two Months Earlier in England

I must have read my uncle's last letter a dozen times and drank endless cups of tea to calm my frayed nerves. As I considered how to get to him before he ceased to exist. After much agonising, I had telephoned Martin, who was at home over the weekend. Martin had been my manager for the past eight and a half years, and we had grown very close. There had even been a rumour going around that Martin and I were having a torrid affair. We both knew differently and decided to intensify the rumour by playing it for all it was worth. Together we had decided I should take my uncle's letter in to work so he could read it for himself. The minute I got into work the following Monday, I asked for a meeting with Martin.

I suggested we had lunch and I would pick up the bill. Martin, however, had other ideas and decided to book a table for two in one of his favourite wine bars-cum-restaurant. We had arrived at the trendy establishment with plenty of time to spare before our meal was served. The minute we were led to our table, I gave Martin no chance whatsoever to get comfortable. I had the letter ready, and I thrusted it into his hand.

"I need your help, Martin. Here's the letter. Read it."

Martin read the letter and drank several glasses of wine in the process.

He ran a finger up and down my arm and exclaimed in his typical theatrical manner, "My poor, poor little darling. You must be beside yourself with worry."

His beautifully manicured hand reached out to stroke my face. From time to time he ran a finger softly down one side of my cheek or blew a kiss or two in my direction. "Oh dear" and "Good heavens" were followed by "Ah ha's" and "Oh no's" as he absorbed the contents of Uncle Daniel's letter.

I wanted six months off work, and Martin and I became locked in negotiations. The emergency meeting held in our department a few weeks ago, was on my mind. At the meeting, it was declared that the management wanted to know whether any members of staff were willing to accept voluntary redundancy. We all knew the real reason behind the redundancy scheme was the fault of the company's promotions department. They'd cocked up again, and the company had been forced to pay out compensations left, right, and centre. Martin knew as well as I that our office was overstaffed. There was no reason for him not to let me go. I put the redundancy idea to him as delicately as I could. To my utter disappointment, Martin gave the idea the briefest consideration and then flatly rejected it.

"I am not prepared to let you go, Sav. It's out of the question! You're a valued member of staff, and you are asking me to help you to leave! This is the same as asking me to help you jump ship. This is preposterous… not to mention disloyal. You shock me, Sav! How could you have thought of such a thing?"

Martin had glanced condescendingly in my direction, picked up his wine glass, and huffed contemptuously; as if brushing Casper's hairs off his cashmere jacket. I wasn't sure whether I should feel ashamed or angry. I was stunned; for I was sure he would have seen things from my angle.

Martin's face had become flushed, and those little white dots appeared on his lips. This meant he was either angry or hurt. I raised an eyebrow at him, giving the impression I was unconcerned. The truth is, I was crying inside and desperately hoping he'd come around to my way of thinking. Even before we had met up, I had hoped Martin had considered this a good idea and even that he might have included me in the list of staff who wanted to go. I had to keep my nerves and remain calm even though I wanted to weep. Martin gave me one of those odd looks of his, then waved his manicured hand dismissively again and returned to the steak on the plate in front of him. I felt frustrated and disappointed, I swore to myself the next time his hand waved dismissively at me I would snap one of his fingers off with my teeth.

Martin seemed to be toying with me in my hour of distress and it irritated me. He just wasn't taking me as seriously as I hoped he would. I pushed my plate away, for I had lost my appetite. I smiled back at him, returning the same odd look that I had learned to mimic to perfection. Then I picked up my wine glass and took a careful sip.

"If I were to do this for you, Savannah, it would be seen as favouritism. I happen to know, there are others who want this redundancy too. Granted, their reasons are different from yours."

I could have leapt across the table and smothered him with big sloppy kisses- when he took up the subject again. Instead, I sat there pushing food around my plate with my fork. I was certain he was enjoying every minute of my agony. Desperation got the better of me now. My wishes took centre stage and my thoughts began to create a revolution in my head. Martin's vivid blue eyes challenged me from across the table.

"I'll give you 'jump ship'… with a dash of disloyalty thrown in for good measures. Keep on tempting me, Martin. Just when have I ever been disloyal? Let's get it out into the open now. …I know how you feel. You see, Martin, with or without your help I'm going!"

Martin leaned across the table and his eyes danced with demonic mischief!

"I just love it when you are angry, Sav. Those oriental brown eyes of yours narrow into a squint. It makes me feel all devilish!"

Martin's hair flopped over his forehead and I waited for him to do the usual elegant toss of his head. I wasn't disappointed. With the slightest of moves his hair fell perfectly into place. I gave him a mocking look for Martin was vainer than the vainest females around.

"You look like a leering schoolboy. You are not having anymore wine," I chided, moving the two bottles of wine to my side of the table.

Martin reached forward to grab the bottles and his unruly locks slid down his forehead again. I reached forward and very carefully pushed his hair back into place, trailing a finger lightly down the bridge of his nose as I did so. He sniffed my neck, then followed me with his eyes as I sat down again.

"Now who's going to do that if you go?" he asked, smothering my hand with wine-induced kisses.

"Only you can reveal that closely-guarded secret, Martin," I said.

Although he and I were close friends and we shared secret things with each other, I had never seen any sign of a partner in Martin's home or otherwise. His private life was a mystery, and it never occurred to me to pry. We were very similar privately. If and when he was ready for me to know, he would tell me. He turned his nose up at my reply and I sneered at him. I decided to ask him a question that had being plaguing my mind for the longest time. With a sniff of a wine glass I summoned the courage to ask.

"Martin, honey, are you in love with me? Just a tiny bit maybe? I'm sometimes confused by your…"

I let out a puff of frustrated air for the words, which I had in my head had deserted me just when I needed them most. That wasn't how I wanted to put the question at all.

"Of course I'm in love with you, Sav. Which man wouldn't? You are very attractive and sweet-natured. You are hugely kind and considerate of others." Then with a wounded look on his sweet face, he added, "I thought you'd never notice."

I felt more confused by this wonderful man than ever. I couldn't say a word and just sat there looking stupid. I glanced at Martin for he too had gone quiet. I noticed his mood had changed to one of thoughtfulness. His hands were clasped together with two fingers resting on his lips. He began leaning his head from side to side. For a moment, I became worried as I noticed the thoughtful look on his face change to one of vulnerability. Then, like a chameleon adjusting to its environment, he changed again.

"My petite little puss, not only do I find you irresistible, I love the way you smell too."

"Ooo… honey I love you too… but then you know that."

This was as far as it was going to go. Having asked the question and got an answer, I had no idea what to do with the information and had no intention of finding out anymore. It was time to move the conversation back on track. Martin's heart condition and his perplexing sexuality was not the reason for our dinner date.

"Martin," I said, "this is madness. You are tipsy and you are gay. In case it escaped your notice, I am a woman. A female."

I changed my tone from teasing now, to reflect the delicate situation I had unwittingly engineered.

"Savannah, I am neither gay nor tipsy, I assure you!" Then, with an expression of distaste he said, "I simply cannot contemplate why people believe I'm gay! Admittedly, I've neither had an encounter with a woman nor with a man for that matter. But does that mean I'm gay or cannot fall in love?"

I placed a finger on my lips. I was stunned, flabbergasted! I felt an absolute idiot for like everyone else at work, I was convinced my darling friend was gay. His admission left me relieved as well as befuddled. He had become the confidant, soul mate, big brother, and all-time friend that had been missing from my world. I loved him dearly as a sister would love a brother. To learn his feelings were respectable was an immense weight off my mind. I was sure that even though he admitted he loved me, his love were not of a sexual nature. Anyway, I just didn't want to know anymore. That settled that, I thought to myself. It was time to move the conversation back where I wanted it.

Earlier, I had sensed Martin knew exactly what he was doing. Either he was never going to include me in the redundancy programme or he would include me and let me go. I often deputised for him in his absence at work, but there were members of the team who were as capable and could easily take over the role. I wondered what he could possibly lose by letting me go. Our friendship, for one, would not alter except that I wouldn't be in London for a while. We would both still be at the end of telephones and could chat whenever we wanted. The only thing that would suffer was our regular dinner dates, which would have to be put on hold. The same would apply too, for the visits we made to each other's homes. Surely my beloved uncle's welfare was far more important than work. Uncle Daniel needed me desperately and I wanted to go to him. My mind was made up and I felt no disloyalty. I grew anxious as I felt Martin would never agree to let me go. The last person I wanted a fight with was dear sweet Martin, but he was leaving me no alternative. If necessary, I was prepared to go over his head. I had to give it one last shot. I blinked and tears rolled down my cheeks. I began to wail.

"I've told you time and again I wanted to leave. I don't enjoy my work anymore. This has no bearing on you. You know I adore you. I'll never be blessed with another boss I can call a true friend. You're unique, Martin... but this is my future we are talking about. This is my life. I cannot desert my responsibilities just because my boss is afraid of loosing me. Things have changed, Martin. Peaceful View's in my blood. Whether you agree or not. I'm going. Don't force me to go over your head... please."

I looked imploringly at him across the table. I stretched my hand out for the neatly folded handkerchief that was perfectly placed in his breast pocket. Martin downed his knife and fork, pushed back his chair, and crossing his legs in that camp way of his, he proceeded to stare at me.

A look of awkwardness replaced the blankness on his face; he blushed. Then, with an expression of utter distaste, he pulled out the handkerchief, shook its perfectly-ironed folds, and handed it to me.

"Sav… you know I am dreadfully fond of you. So much so…I would readily run off with you. However, my fondness does not alter the fact I want that back washed, neatly pressed, and folded as it is now!" With two dainty fingers, Martin shook the handkerchief free of its perfectly ironed folds. He handed it to me.

"Thank you, Martin," I said. I caught sight of my reflection in the mirrored walls. "Ooo… I look a terrible sight," I added, sniffing into his sweet-smelling hanky.

There I was fighting for my release from a job that in my opinion had become a life sentence. In the process, I had embarrassed myself and, no doubt, embarrassed Martin too. Yet all the time, this complex man was only concerned with his initialled blooming handkerchief! If Martin's multifarious personality had me baffled at times, I saw a potential minefield where his sexuality was concerned. I had to console myself with the thought that only Martin could be more intricate than life itself. And only Martin could be disquieted by the thought of a nose being blown into his hanky. I nodded in agreement to the terms of the hanky loan! Then I blew my nose once again – just to rile him.

I thought I heard Martin speak as he stabbed a tipsy finger into his chest and peered at me over the top of his trendy purple spectacles. His manicured fingers twisted his wine glass as if he was mulling over something life-changing. I looked inquiringly at him but all he did was continue to peer at me with an expression I couldn't read. I opened my mouth with the intention of asking him a question regarding what I thought I heard him say, but I shut my mouth again. Then I couldn't stand the suspense any longer. I had to ask.

"Did you say something, Martin?"

I sniffed into his hanky again and he frowned in distaste at me.

"I said, Savannah, it is done!"

Gone was his usual "Sav" – the name he called me by both at work and privately! This told me I had disappointed him somehow.

"It is done? What is done, Martin?" I asked, twitching my nose for the tears had made it dry and tight.

"You want to take the voluntary redundancy package, don't you?"

"Ye-yes, I do."

"Then it's done."

I found it difficult coming to grips with what I heard. I wasn't going to ask anymore questions, though. I desperately wanted to get out of my job and to get away. There was so much I wanted to do, and I could only accomplish them by returning to Peaceful View.

"Thank you, Martin… thank you," I cried, sniffing again. "I'll make this up to you, I promise."

Words weren't enough to show Martin my gratitude even though he had made me squirm and I had embarrassed us both in the process.

"Oh, you'll make it up to me? Don't you worry your pretty little head on that score. I shall be your first guest. Don't expect me to pay a single penny!" he said with another brisk look in my direction, which I knew was pretentious.

"It's dollars actually…" I said, cheekily. "As if I'd let you pay anyway."

I blew him a kiss through tears of joy. I simply couldn't believe my change of fortune. I was beside myself and my excitement mounted. I pinched myself as I took a wee glimpse into my new life. Martin's foot prodded mine under the table and my excitement cooled temporarily.

My eyes followed the direction Martin's travelled. I was horrified to find we had attracted quite an audience. Every pair of eyes looked curiously in our direction!

"Oooo… how embarrassing!" I whispered as I tried to shrink smaller than my five feet one inch.

"Now look here, Savannah. Get into the little girls room and clean up your face," Martin ordered.

I ignored him and picked up my glass instead. I wasn't going to run in shame because curious eyes were trained on us.

"Can't we celebrate? Just one sip of wine first… please?" I petitioned.

"Sav, we have an audience. For Pete's sake, it's embarrassing."

I looked around again. This time, I did not hide the fact I was looking back at the prying faces.

To our far right was a table with two women. I was certain one of them was trying her best to get Martin to notice her. How brazenly flirtatious, I thought. For all she knew, I was his wife. Do women no longer have morals or decorum? I asked myself. Still, I wasn't going to walk the moral highroad for this was the opportunity I needed. I grabbed it with both hands.

"Martin, honey," I said, "don't look now. But over to our right two gorgeous ladies are eyeing you up. I'm sure the brunette is trying to get your attention!"

"Just because I'm in love with you doesn't mean I want… you know what I mean!" This was the first time I've seen him lost for words. Martin's face registered revulsion at the thought and I decided to tease him just a tad more.

"What's wrong with her? She looks perfectly lovely to me," I stated.

I looked across at another table where six boisterous ladies were squeaking and squawking their way through several bottles of wine. They were obviously celebrating something and were all drunk. Twice the manager had approached their table and asked them to be quiet. Martin's eyes followed mine.

"Now stop it, you cat!" Martin said in his uproarious camp manner.

I burst out laughing, forgetting I had just taken a mouthful from my glass. Martin and the white tablecloth were covered in sprays of deep red! He glared at me with pursed lips. I sucked on a finger to prevent me from dissolving into hilarity – for if I did so, it would be riotous and that would never do.

"I never could stand to see a woman cry. And I can't stand one who spills exquisite wine regardless of how she chooses to spill it."

He picked up a napkin and began to mop up the wine, which had, unfortunately, ended up on his face and hands too!

"Now, now. Who's being catty?" I said, but Martin was still on planet Martin! "It reminds me of my poor mother's suffering at the hands of my cruel father!" Martin's referral to his mother soon sobered me up. All I needed now; was for him to start talking about Casper, his pampered pooch. He never talked about his mother very much for it seemed memories of her made him sad. More than once I had seen him dusting her photographs with sadness etched on his loveable face.

Having opened up more than one can of worms in Martin's life, maybe it was time to head off to the ladies. "You've ruined our meal! We might as well call for desserts. Now pull yourself together. I'm going to the little boy's room. You have five minutes to replace that winning smile of yours. I want to see it when I walk back through that door."

He indicated by way of his head the door to the gents'. Then he looked at me thoughtfully for a second or two and sarcastically added, "On second thought, take ten minutes. You look like cold mashed potatoes."

"Thank you, my sweet. So eloquently put!"

I wiped a finger across my moist eyes.

"Yes… you do look a mess!" he replied dryly!

I raised an eyebrow in mocked surprise at him.

"I just knew you would assure me. I love you too!"

I creased my mascara-stained face into a smile, stuck my nose into the air, and followed him out.

CHAPTER 9

Martin had a way of either turning the most serious issues into a pantomime or reducing you to tears with his dry wit and caustic tongue. However, I never got too upset with him, for he was a truly beautiful human being both inside and out. He was a natural whenever a crisis arose and he often turned the crisis into a comedy show. Though tonight he had made me suffer, I wouldn't hold it against him; somewhere in his psyche, he had a valid reason. I refreshed my face and re-applied a light touch of makeup along with a little lipstick and mascara. I inspected my reflection in the mirror and was satisfied I looked presentable. I opened the door and found Martin waiting for me. I took his arm and kissed his cheek. He had removed all traces of wine from his face.

He placed a hand over mine and whispered wickedly into my ear, "Now dazzle the curious eyes with your beautiful smile, darling."

I smiled regally as we walked back to our table and took our seats once again. Our tablecloth had been changed and a fresh yellow rose placed in the single-stemmed vase on our table. Soon our desserts arrived and were placed in front of us.

The minute the young waitress had left our table, Martin said, "Sav, darling, I have a confession to make!"

At this, my brain stalled for I had stopped breathing and my heart did several double flips. I had already learned Martin wasn't gay after all. He hated to see a woman cry and was in love with me. I couldn't think what it was he planned to unleash now. What more could there possibly be? I wondered. Convinced Martin was about to tell me there was no redundancy package and the whole exercise was a joke. I broke into hot sweats. I wasn't even given the chance to discover the dreams I nurtured in the depths of my heart, for my body suddenly decided menopause was the safest option. Was I ever going to experience the wonders of falling hopelessly in love before my entire bodily function shut down on me? It seemed the answer was no. My skin began to crawl as if I had been dragged through stinging nettles. I poked a finger into one ear and wiggled it furiously, and then I did the same to the other ear. I checked my nail for wax, but my finger was clean. Satisfied there were no obstructions in my ear ways, I prepared myself for the worse. With both elbows resting on the table, I propped up my face in the crock of my palms and looked searchingly into his face.

"Sav, I'd put your name on the redundancy list two weeks ago!"

I shoved a massive mouthful of chocolate moose cake into my mouth as I felt my face frowning. I immediately relaxed my muscles, for the last thing I wanted was awful facial lines in addition to premature menopause! I shovelled another forkful into my mouth and exhaled noisily. Martin re-filled our wine glasses, and my hand slid over the tablecloth towards my glass. I picked it up and raised it to my lips, but, instead of sipping the wine, I drank it down as if it were a tumbler of water.

"Martin... you'd done... what?" I asked, picking up the bottle of wine to pour myself another glass.

"I'll do that, Sav. Give me that bottle, please."

Martin's face was flushed; he looked demandingly at me. I complied by pushing the bottle towards him.

"I wasn't going to spill any... you know," I murmured.

Why

"I won't take that chance. You drank a whole glass in one swallow."

My left hand reached up to stroke my throat.

"You're not going to be sick, are you, Sav?"

Now it was Martin that looked like yesterday's mashed potatoes. He turned a nasty shade of grey fearing I was going to disgrace us both by throwing up. Tonight, though, my delicate stomach was holding out. If I was wearing a hat, I'd raise it to my stomach. Drink wise, I told myself. My metabolism was behaving impeccably. I held my breath again and looked intently at Martin.

"Martin… then why did you allow me to make a prized monkey of myself?" I asked. He pretended not to hear me. He began a to-do with his napkin, tucking it down his shirt collar before scooping a dainty amount of chocolate moose into his mouth. I huffed and puffed to get his attention. Finally, he reached across the table for my hand.

"This chocolate moose cake is simply divine. It's your recipe, isn't it, Sav?"

"Dunno," I said, still studying his face.

"I'd given Steve the recipe. You'd brought him to dinner at my place. He was impressed with it, so… who knows. Why don't you ask him? He's your friend," I said, a little cheesed off.

I wasn't concerned either way. I retrieved my hand from his and folded my arms. It seemed I hardly knew Martin; he was more complex than a rubic cube.

"Patience, Sav, my sweet, is a virtue. Unfortunately, it's not one of your many endearing attributes. I wanted to teach you patience, for if you are going to run your ancestral home as a going concern, you will have to learn patience real quick! The other reason is that I'm going to miss you terribly." I pursed my lips for I was going to cry again and I didn't want to. I simply couldn't embarrass us again. Twice in one night would be too much. My emotions were hovering on the brink. I was overwhelmed by Martin and I was going to miss him very much. He took my hand again. "I wanted to be sure too. You are certain this is what you want to do?"

"Oh… I don't know what to say. I'm going to cry unless you shut up!."

"Don't you dare! I am warning you."

I lent over the table and pulled Martin into my arms. I could have hugged him and never let go.

"My big six-foot marshmallow of a darling! You're all soft behind that po-faced facade you show to the world," I whispered into his ear.

"And what is that supposed to mean, Savannah?" Out went Sav and in came Savannah again! "I might have to propose to you for I will miss you terribly."

We held on to each other as if it was going to be the last time.

Two weeks later, my favourite security guard locked the large iron gates behind me for the last time. I looked back at the sprawling building, knowing I was never going to return. In my handbag, I had a cheque so handsomely generous, it exceeded all my expectations. In the bags that hung from both my arms and those in the boot of Martin's sports car, were bottles of very expensive perfumes and wines. I hadn't opened all the presents I had been given and had no idea what was in those packages. My stomach bubbled with excitement for I was about to begin a new life in a place I adored. Martin had promised to join me there over the holiday period. What more could I possibly have asked for except to enjoy my many blessings with a dash of good health and a happy ever after?

******

I had walked all the way with my head bowed, my mind focused on the last few weeks. Looking up towards the hill ahead of us, I saw Aunt Eva's white-painted house. Sitting on top of the hill, It stood stark under an overcast sky. Uncle Daniel and Bobby chatted throughout the journey and, at times, tried to include me, but I was having none of it. I was wrapped up in my own thoughts. As we approached the front gardens, I saw two women, whom I had heard about from Bobby, sitting on the veranda engrossed in a lively hand-gesturing tête-à-tête. They looked at ease. They did not get up to meet us and instead carried on their conversation until we were standing directly in front of the veranda.

"Look, Yvette, here comes Syke and Trim!"

I recalled the expression, which meant "two of a kind", or "inseparable friends". One of the women in particular seemed awfully familiar with Uncle Daniel. I found, to my surprise, I resented this!

"We wondered where you two had disappeared to," the familiar one said, folding her arms in mocked vexation.

"I take it everything is in order then, ladies?" Uncle Daniel asked putting the box down on the veranda step.

"Oh yes. Everything is just perfect," they answered in unison.

Then the familiar one charged energetically down the veranda steps. Her ample breasts heaving like a couple of water-filled balloons. I stepped aside to give her and her breast enough room.

She reached the last step and exclaimed, "Lord above! It's Miss Savannah. I would recognise that round face and Chinese eyes anywhere in the world."

She flung her arms wide to emphasize the word "world." Then she squared up to my uncle with hands on hips in mock confrontation. I watched the performance unfolding before my eyes with a mix of jealousy and distaste. I positively disliked this overexcited woman and her full-to-overflowing chest.

"Daniel… you never breathed a word Miss Savannah was here?" she said, pushing her face close to his.

I closed my eyes for I couldn't contemplate my uncle in a clinch with this "wench," as Grandma would have called her.

"Ellen, my niece's presence on Peaceful View is my business not yours. Don't concern yourself," said Uncle Daniel. He sat down next to the box he had carried from the summer house.

He lit a cigar, inhaled, and blew the smoke at Ellen. I looked around for Bobby and saw him coming out of the house with a bottle of Red Stripe beer in one hand. I made a questioning face at him and he mouthed the words, "girlfriend!" I disliked this woman even more now my suspicions were confirmed. Grandma would never have tolerated her. It wouldn't be long before I got rid of her. I would see her off so fast, it would be as if a rocket had been lit under her!

Uncle Daniel reached up and squeezed my arm; he must have noticed the look on my face. I most certainly wasn't pleased and was certain that my displeasure was clear for all to see.

I hugged him and, making sure no one else could hear, I whispered into his ear, "Get rid of her."

He looked up into my face, and I made sure he understood me. I maintained the same frosty ice-maiden look on my face.

"Go on into the house, princess. Bobby will show you around. When you have freshened up, I'll come and find you."

Out of the good manners I had been taught by my grandmother, I nodded acknowledgement in the direction of the familiar one and her sister. For now, I would leave Uncle Daniel to enjoy her company. I followed Bobby into the house in search of my luggage and a much-needed bathroom.

Bobby told me to wonder around the house to familiarise myself with the layout. But after I had found myself at the same starting point twice, I gave up and concentrated on opening doors until I found a bathroom. Eventually, I found one set between two bedrooms along a narrow hall. This bathroom had two doors! One connected with another bedroom as an en suite. I had no complaints; the bathroom was ample for its purpose. I was looking forward to a thorough scrub, which I needed desperately. I turned on the hot tap and heard some sort of engine kicked into action somewhere. After a time, I figured the engine sound was a generator – I had much to catch up on. I frowned at my forgetfulness. The bathtub was designed for two and would take a while to fill to the depth I desired. I gauged the flow of water and went off to find Bobby and my luggage. As I stepped out onto the corridor, I collided with him sandwiched between two suitcases and my rucksack strung over his shoulder. I began to laugh as I watched him struggling. He most definitely wasn't used to hard work. I had felt his hands in the summer house and they were way softer than my own!

"Hi there. I was just coming to find you," I said.

I was glad to bump into him for I had had enough of loosing myself in ugly Aunt Eva's house.

"Are you finding your way around alright?" he asked me cheerily.

"No. I got lost. There are a lot of changes. It's different – bigger. I'm glad I found you."

"You remember Ruby, Aunt Eva's daughter, don't you, Savannah?"

"Yes – though I probably wouldn't recognise her now,"

I linked my arm into Bobby's, and he led me along the corridor.

"Over the years, Ruby had the place upgraded. It has just kind of… grown," Bobby explained as we came to a halt in front of one of the rooms halfway down the corridor.

"This is Aunt Eva's bedroom, Savannah…I mean… was."

He opened the door, and my heart sank to the shiny floor. I imagined my aunt appearing in the dead of night dressed in her burial attire. Her hideously ugly features still intact, and demanding I leave her bedroom instantly! I turned around and walloped Bobby.

"Forget it. I'm not sleeping in that room. What is this? A continuation of my nightmare? Don't even think of putting my cases in there. Get the rest of my things out of there right now!" I demanded.

I kicked him in the leg and then fold my arms in vexation. I used to feel sorry for my aunt when I was small, but that wasn't good enough reason to sleep in her bedroom. I could almost see her in front of me. Earlier when I was searching for the bathroom, I had opened that very door and had quickly slammed it shut again seeing her ugly features smiling out at me from the wall – had left me cold!

"Savannah, I'm right next door and Uncle D is on the other side of you. You're in this room because it's between us both."

I couldn't give a fiddler's fart. I wasn't sleeping in that room.

"Get my things out!"

"Savannah, if you need us in the middle of the night, we will be right next-door to you."

I exhaled impatiently, for words had escaped me. I did not for a single second believe Bobby's reasoning. Why on earth would I need anyone in the middle of the night? Had I been disabled?

"I give not a fig for what you thought. I would rather head back to the summer house or the branch of a tree. So you better hear me, or I swear you'll wear your testicles hanging from your earlobes!"

I positioned myself to stand right in front of him, ready to jam my kneecap right where the sun doesn't shine.

"OK... I'll go and get Uncle D. Wait here," he said, after much hesitation.

I did not believe Uncle Daniel would have settled me in Aunt Eva's old bedroom. This was Bobby's idea. I could feel his sickening motive through the very walls. It was a very bad joke, and I wasn't pleased at all. In fact, the thought of sleeping in Aunt Eva's room was more disconcerting than the threat to my life.

"Ooo...no. I'm coming with you."

I followed him out into the corridor and into the kitchen where Uncle Daniel was busy preparing vegetables at the kitchen sink.

"We have a problem, Uncle D. Savannah refuses to stay in Aunt Eva's old bedroom," Bobby said, looking at Uncle Daniel as if I was causing them grave hardship.

"Bob, there's eight bedrooms in the house. Savannah can have her pick of rooms," Uncle Daniel said.

I scoffed disdainfully at Bobby. I needed proof the choice of rooms was his idea and here it was.

"Savannah, you can have the rooms Ruby uses when she is here. I'll swap you over when I get a chance. Is that alright, princess?"

I nodded, for I did not care which room I was given, so long as it wasn't my ugly Aunt Eva's.

"Uncle D, we agreed Savannah would stay in Aunt Eva's room. It's near us both. It's a big room and it looks out onto the mountains she loves."

Bobby argued - determined it seems, I accept the bedroom he had chosen for me. It was as if I wasn't there and had no voice of my own. I glared at my uncle.

"Bobby, the choice of rooms was your idea… and you are not hearing me. Savannah's not happy with that room. She's been through enough since coming home. Move her luggage to Ruby's rooms. I'll be along to give you a hand in a minute."

I grinned in triumph at Bobby who turned and sneaked out of the kitchen. I was in no doubt I saw disappointment on Bobby's face.

"Savannah, you seem to have left me. What are you thinking about?" Uncle Daniel asked.

I drew a sudden breath and walked over to where he stood by the kitchen sink. I reached up and touched his swollen face.

"Come now. What's the reason for the long face? Eva's bedroom wasn't such a bad idea, you know. Bobby thought it would have been ideal as we would be on either side of you."

He pulled out a chair from under the kitchen table, sat down, and slapped his knee for me to sit on. Instead, I walked around the back of the chair and wrapped my arms around his neck the way I used to do as a child.

"Tell me what's wrong," he persisted.

I didn't want to trouble him at this time, but his probing voice made it so very hard.

"Well," I said, "I'm not superstitious or anything, but Aunt Eva is different. She was not exactly… you know. Her room has photographs of her. I'd opened the door when I was searching for a bathroom. I couldn't stay in there with her watching me. It's a shrine… ….full of her ugly mug. It's morbid. I need time to get used to that face again!" I said, hoping I didn't sound cruel nor be damned for speaking ill of the dead.

Uncle Daniel turned his head away and his body began to shake spasmodically. Then he lurched forward and doubled over, laughing. Another voice joined in, and the laughing itch trickled through the house. I looked out and saw Bobby standing in the corridor. It seemed he had been there all along. His belly-wrenching laughter merged with Uncle Daniel's, and I suddenly remembered the bath I had left running!

"Aunt Eva was truly beaten with the ugly stick!" Bobby said, stuttering and slurring his words through fits of laughter.

"My sister… my poor sister. God rest her soul, she was ugly!" Uncle Daniel howled again.

I dashed from the kitchen and down the corridor.

CHAPTER 10

I turned the water off just before it began cascading over the sides of the huge tub. Then I gathered my composure, for I, too, had caught the laughing itch as images of my ugly Aunt Eva came back. Now I needed bits and pieces from the boxes I had brought with me. I went back to the kitchen.

"Can I have a knife, please? I need to open one of the boxes. You two can come with me."

I followed behind Bobby and Uncle Daniel led the way back along the corridor. Although my suitcase had been moved across to the bedroom I was going to have instead of Aunt Eva's, the boxes I had brought with me were left behind in her bedroom.

"You two go in. I'll wait here."

Bobby's eyes found mine, and the instant our eyes locked I knew instinctively that Bobby was thinking about the same ghastly memory as me. I pushed him forward.

Ever since the day I was forced to leave my grandmother's custody and was packed off to England to a father I did not know; I dreamed of the day I would return. Nevertheless, memories of a haunting kind prevented me from returning. But I knew if I was ever going to free myself from the memories that had me chained to the past, I would have to face each one regardless of how unpalatable they might be. Finally, I could postpone my return no longer. My uncle's plight compelled me to come home. Now, however, my return to this beautiful island grew more disconcerting as the minutes ticked by. The cruelty I suffered as a child, as well as my childhood misdemeanours, came flooding back. I decided to bite the bullet and confront the most disturbing demon of them all.

"Uncle Daniel, there's something we need to tell you. Bobby and I have a confession to make. We better go back into the kitchen,"

That inner voice that guides my conscience caused the words to tumble out. But the moment I opened my mouth, I regretted my decision to confess my most disturbing misdemeanours.

Uncle Daniel surveyed Bobby with narrowed eyes. I guessed he thought Bobby had told me the truth about the fire and the threat to my life – things, he had expressly asked Bobby not to tell me. The three of us turned and walked sombrely back into the kitchen.

"Why don't you sit here, Uncle D?" Bobby said, patting the back of one of Aunt Eva's curiously large armchairs. Uncle Daniel walked grimly to the chair, sat down, and crossed his gangly legs in his trademark fashion. Bobby stood directly behind the chair Uncle Daniel sat in, and I sat in one of the dining chairs opposite them. I fidgeted on the chair and thought if they weren't so superbly carved, I would swear Aunt Eva had made them herself. They were terribly hard and uncomfortable and forced a person to sit in an unyielding position. I wouldn't be surprised if, when I finally got up, I would have to gather my skin up off the chair.

"Why do I get a bad feeling about this?" Uncle Daniel said, as he pulled a cigar from his breast pocket and struck a match. His voice wrenched my attention away from the chair and back to the confession.

I pursed my lips the way Dick had taught me to do, pulling them together and stretching them as far forward as I could. This forced my neck forward, and I began to prod the veins protruding under the skin on my neck.

"Uncle D, believe me, it's not what you think."

Bobby tried to reassure Uncle Daniel while I sat quietly evaluating my cousin. Uncle Daniel obviously believed Bobby had said something to me, and it was clear that Bobby thought nothing of lying to him. Much eye searching went on between them until Uncle Daniel relented and nodded rigidly. He then cast a side-eyed glance at me as I struggled to find a place on the chair that wouldn't leave me, black and blue.

"Bobby, are you going to tell Uncle Daniel or should I?" I asked, wanting to get it over with as fast as possible.

Having carried this extraordinary secret since I was eight years old, I wanted to rid myself of it once and for all. This was no ordinary childhood prank; it was a profoundly evil deed.

"I'm cool, Savannah. Go ahead. If you miss anything out, I'll fill in."

"Agreed," I said.

Bobby walked over to stand behind my chair.

"Uncle Daniel, do you remember what happened on the night of Aunt Rhonda's wake?" I asked, Getting straight to the point.

"Ye-es, I remember," he said, with a firm nod of his head.

"Good… that's a start," I said, as guilt, shame, and bitter regret passed like a cloud over my heart.

I couldn't have felt more unsettled as I did now. How we could have done what we did at such tender years, beggars belief. I had spent years fearing Pastor Mac's prediction of my future in hell until I discovered, by chance, it was all a lie told by so called heads of Christ on earth. Both the Catholic and Anglican churches along with others teach this vile doctrine. To my utter relief I found evidence in the Bible, which describes mankind's grave as hell.

There was no fiery abyss presided over by the devil and no place of eternal torment for men who tripped over the boundaries of the Ten Commandments. I was relieved to read I could be forgiven for my sins. I had prayed persistently; asking God to take away the guilt I carried for what I had done that night. In order for me to truly move on from this memory; confessing what I had done was the right thing to do, or so I thought.

"What about it, Savannah?" Uncle Daniel asked. I looked at him through a fog of smoke. He studied me for a while and began a finger-tapping action on the arm of the chair. "Are you still afraid of the old goat, Savannah?"

"One question at a time… please. This is not easy. And yes, I'm afraid… but my fear comes from what I did on the night of her wake."

"I see," Uncle Daniel looked now at Bobby then absently spoke to himself, "Well, I never!"

"Me, Bobby, Lilly, and Betty… sort of… did something abnormal to her." I blurted out. I stabbed Bobby with my elbow for he had decided to sit next to me.

"Uncle D… did anyone ever mention something peculiar happening to Aunt Rhonda's corpse?"

Bobby asked the question so barefacedly; I covered my face with my hands. The word "corpse", to my mind, was far worse than the word "body". The times I had looked back on what we had done and wished I could turn the clock back were just too many to count.

"Well," Uncle Daniel replied as puffs of his cigar smoke spread a foul smell around the kitchen.

As I watched the smoke swirl around and climb upwards, a sense of shame made me wish I could shrink myself into oblivion.

"Yes? Well, what?" enquired Bobby far too impatiently.

"As it goes… something odd… if not macabre… happened. It was a mystery."

Uncle Daniel uncrossed his legs and stood up. He walked around the back of the chair he had sat in a moment or two ago. Then from this position he proceeded to stare at us through what appeared to be disbelieving eyes. I drew my shoulders upward to hide my face, and then pulled my neck down into them.

"Go on, I'm listening," said Uncle Daniel.

"We did it, Uncle D," said Bobby brazenly.

"We? Who did what, Bobby?" Uncle Daniel's once-appealing chestnut eyes suddenly took on a new lease of life.

They positively sparkled with curiosity or perhaps disgust. I was convinced Uncle Daniel had got the picture before we even began to paint it for him! I stood up with all intention of running from the room. I turned slowly towards the doorway.

"Sit down, Savannah," ordered Uncle Daniel, and I sat down again.

Bobby continued, "We – meaning Savannah, me, Lilly, and Betty. We did it."

I noticed my name was the first to be called. The spineless coward! I thought to myself. He darted behind my chair as if trying to hide. I made a funny face at Uncle Daniel in a bid to lighten the mood. He didn't seem to notice; his attention had shifted to the kitchen floor as he paced around us with thoughtful steps.

"Interesting story," he finally said as he turned his attention on the stove.

He began stirring and sampling the food he was cooking. I observed him from behind and saw his shoulders shaking ever so slightly. I thought he must be recalling the spectacle that had greeted them all, when each one had filed in to pay their last respects to great Aunt Rhonda. I decided to make enquiries about dinner:

"Uncle Daniel, what's for dinner? That smells scrumptious! My mouth is watering already."

"Never mind the smells and your watering mouth. Dinner can wait until after you two have finished this story," he said determinedly.

There was no getting out of this one now for sure, I thought. Uncle Daniel stood with his back to the sink and was facing us again. He put his hand up to stroke his beard, and then seemed to remember it was no longer there.

"Well," continued Bobby, "Aunt Rhonda died, as you know. When we heard the news, Savannah, Lilly, Betty, and me whooped with joy. She was a mean old witch. She hated everyone, especially us, children. She fought with everyone in the family… even her own children and grandchildren. Her husband ran away and left her after years of abuse. She was jealous of her relatives and constantly caused bad feelings amongst all. She used to whack us spitefully if we so much as picked up a fallen fruit from under her fruit trees. She would make us drop the fruits and force us to watch her crush them under the soles of her big water boot. Her evil grey-blue eyes would penetrate ours at the same time." The passion in Bobby's voice told me, he had not repented nor had he gotten over his resentment of Aunt Rhonda. He stuffed both his hands in his pockets as he continued to relate our disturbing secret. "She always carried that damn bamboo pole of hers and would swipe violently at us… never caring whether she was inflicting pain. In fact, she used to laugh with every blow. She once hit Betty and me so dammed hard; we were off school for days. That witch broke Betty's arm and sprained my foot! Uncle D… do you remember… ?"

Bobby took a rain check to examine his bare feet as if he could feel the pain through them. It seemed that particular beating remained a sore point.

"Yes, Bobby, I remember quite well. It was I who went to get the good doctor."

"Without warning, the old mare kicked the bucket… just like that."

Bobby snapped his fingers to add emphasis to the sudden passing of great Aunt Rhonda, and Uncle Daniel suppressed his laughter by pretending he had sneezed. Meanwhile, Bobby had completed the examination of his bare feet and now stood in the centre of the arch between the kitchen and the dining room. How he had got to the other end of the kitchen, I didn't know for I was sure he was still hiding behind my chair. "Savannah, help me out, will you, please?"

Suddenly he went and dragged me straight back into the confession. He headed back behind my chair, and I was forced to wade through Aunt Rhonda's cobweb-like ghost that stood in front of my eyes. I ran both my hands over my shame-filled face as if wiping the memory away from before me. Then Uncle Daniel proved to be my savoir.

He gave me more time to get myself ready, and then he asked, "Bobby, people don't give notice before they die. Did you expect the old goat to tell the four of you she was about to kick the bucket?"

I very nearly burst into fits of laughter at Uncle Daniel's question. I eyed him discreetly; I wasn't sure how he would react when we finished telling the story. What I was sure of, though, was he had a pretty good idea of the story's ending. My unique family had a bizarre sense of humour and a tendency to see something funny in everything. But then this was no ordinary "run of the mill story", as Grandma would have said. What worried me most was how my uncle would view his little princess from here on. He was waiting for me to begin.

"Oooo… fiddlesticks. I can't do this anymore. I have a right to withdraw my confession, Uncle Daniel, please?" I pleaded, looking to my uncle to rescue me.

Why

"I don't think so, Savannah. I overrule that right. Pick up where your cousin left off, will you?"

The self-appointed judge spoke and I stood condemned for a confession I wished I hadn't started.

"Ooooooh shoot," I said, hugging myself and looking around the room for a quick escape route. How I could do with my darling Martin right this minute. His theatrical character would solve this dilemma straight away. Why, he'd turn the whole thing into a blooming pantomime. "Oh, pumps! I forgot to call Martin to let him know I arrived safely," I said, scratching my head like it was infested with fleas.

"We will come back to Martin in a while, Savannah. Get on with your confession." The self-appointed judge nodded in my direction.

"I really don't want to do this anymore," I wailed. "Uncle Daniel… can't we just forget about it…for you very well know it was us who desecrated Aunt Rhonda's dead body!"

He shook his head.

"No. It was you who wanted to confess. Besides, confession is good for the soul. Carry on, princess."

"Yeah, right," I said, for if I were his princess, he wouldn't make me relate the whole gory details.

I was getting edgy and more than a little browned off with myself. Who says honesty is the best policy? Right now I wanted to string up the person who first uttered those words. Then again, it was my conscience, which drove me to volunteer a confession I had no hope of getting out of.

"Whose soul?" I said, casting a desperate look at my uncle.

My soul, at that moment, was threatening to do a runner. Uncle Daniel fixed softened eyes on me, and I hoped he was about to spare me. As a child, I had always being able to twist him around my little finger. Would it work now? I wondered. I gave him one of my "help me please" looks and waited to hear him say, "All right, Savannah, you don't have to do anything you don't want to do." But it never came. I gave up and unwillingly began again.

"OK. It would have helped if we knew the wretched old bat was going to die."

"Why is that, Savannah?" asked Uncle Daniel.

I ignored him. What I was about to relate, would explain everything. I had no option now but to transport the whole haunting episode back into my mind. I stared straight ahead of me as, bit by bit; I proceeded to resurrect the memories of the devil.

"It wasn't fair. We had been planning to get our own back on the old sow for a long time. Then, she decided to drop dead without warning." I shook my shoulders as if dodging a stroke from Aunt Rhonda's bamboo pole. "Anyway, I had snatched the bamboo pole from her a few days earlier. I was going to batter her with it at the time but decided to run off with it instead. I hid it in the meadow where she wouldn't find it." I switched my focus to Ruby's photograph on the wall in front of me. I wondered how an aunt as repugnantly ugly as Aunt Eva was, could have given birth to such a beauty. Ruby had doll-like features, a tiny mouth, striking eyes, and a sculptured little chin. In contrast, her mother, Aunt Eva's face was nothing short of a creation straight out of Dr Frankenstein's laboratory! She was terribly ugly. "Uncle Daniel, do you ever wonder how ugly Aunt Eva managed to have such a stunning daughter as Ruby? Look at Ruby's photo hanging on the wall. Anyone walking into this house not knowing Aunt Eva was her mother would surely not believe. I think God had pitied her and gave her Ruby in compensation."

"Bravo, Savannah! What an observation. But you are straying, my princess. Stay on track, eh?"

I began to massage my scalp, for it seemed every flea on the island had heard I had come home and had decided to move in on my head! I could swear a battalion of creepy-crawlies were marching through my hair. A last furious scratch, and I left the creepy-crawlies to get on with it.

"On the evening of the old sow's wake, I strolled downhill to her house. I'd picked up the bamboo pole on my way down... along with some ropes Bobby and I had stolen from the shed in the pastures. I propped up the bamboo pole outside the old bat's bedroom window when I got there. Then I went in search of Lilly and Betty. People had started arriving at the house, and those already there were in little groups talking in hushed voices. I found Lilly and Betty, and we were going to meet Bobby when I heard someone say, "Aunt Rhonda's soul was going straight to hell and that she should shovel the coals to heat the furnace for her own roasting!"

"Let me get this straight," said Uncle Daniel, cutting in. "All four of you had planned to take revenge even though the old goat was dead?"

"Yes… dead or alive… she had it coming. Just listen, will you? This is hard enough without you butting in, All four of us had grievances against Aunt Rhonda. We had planned to get her. When the news came to us at school she had passed on, I suggested we beat her up anyway. I already had her bamboo pole, and we decided it was the best weapon to use on her."

I drew a sharp breath, for Aunt Rhonda's face loomed in front of my eyes. Desperate to get rid of her evil image, I rubbed furiously at my eyes and hoped I would have an asthma attack before reaching the end.

"Go on," Bobby urged.

I took this opportunity to pull him from his hiding place behind my chair. I plonked him down to sit next to me, as if his sitting beside me was going to wipe Aunt Rhonda's memory from my mind. I sniggered inwardly and took a side-eyed glance at Uncle Daniel. He sat waiting, hanging on to my every word.

"Even though the evil witch was dead, we were still terrified of her. We began to compare her with Aunt Penny"

I wanted to run from the room but was too afraid to do so just in case I bumped into either Aunt Eva or Aunt Rhonda in the corridor!

"Savannah, do you want me to carry on with the story?" Bobby asked, putting an arm around me. I shook him off me.

"No. As much as I hate this, I must do it. Thanks anyway." I picked up the story again. "We debated who should go in and check she was really dead. We were afraid she might suddenly decide to wake up and start screaming like Aunt Penny had done. It was possible… the same thing could happen. Aunt Penny woke up screaming the first time. The second time… the coffin was halfway down into the grave when her brother thought he heard scratching sounds." I turned to Uncle Daniel and said, "You and some others were lowering Aunt Penny's coffin into the grave. You dropped it and ran off, remember? It was Uncle Harry who'd frantically wrenched open the coffin and pulled a half-dead Aunt Penny out."

Bobby threw himself forward. His face flushed from covert laughter. Uncle Daniel's knees had buckled. He was bent over into an embryonic position on the kitchen floor and was braying like a donkey on heat. I sat with my eyes firmly fixed on Ruby's photograph.

CHAPTER 11

I couldn't figure out how Aunt Eva had managed it for the man she had married was an equally ugly and sour-faced old soul. He had only one useful eye and there were scabs all over his legs. He walked with a stick and sat around under the shade of trees from morning until bedtime. His only interests in life were his possessions, which consisted of a vast herd of sheep and some eighty acres of land, which he leased out to local farmers. He owned a stubborn old mule named Horace and a three-bedroom house in which he lived a contentious life with my Aunt Eva. None of us liked him. He had taken a particular dislike to me after I had asked him whether it was true "he had lost his sight after Horace broke wind in his face." I had heard the story being discussed and wasn't supposed to repeat it. But, as always, my curiosity controlled my actions. However, I never found out if this was truth or just another of the many fables I had heard as a child. I suspected, it was the latter. I sighed. How innocent we are as children, I thought to myself.

"I want to get this over with as quickly as possible," I said, continuing, for Uncle Daniel and Bobby were still hooting around me. "We thought the same thing might happen in Aunt Rhonda's case. But none of us wanted to go into the house to check."

Uncle Daniel interrupted my flow yet again.

"It was the custom in those days to sit with the dead – taking turns to read passages from the Bible until daybreak. Was no one with the old goat?"

I looked at my uncle as if he'd just arrived from outer space. Surely, Uncle Daniel must remember no one would volunteer to sit with Aunt Rhonda's body. Her own children and grandchildren had refused. The dreaded Mr Miller, who would turn up uninvited at every event; to fill his bottomless pit of a belly - and eat everything that wasn't nailed down had refused even! He had complained that he had been insulted! Aunt Rhonda had not a single friend in the world. She had lain stone dead in her big brass bed with only candle lights to keep her company. I ignored my uncle's question again.

"I came up with the idea we'd all squeezed through the doorway at the same time. We climbed up the steps to the front door, hardly daring to breathe. Our arms were tightly linked together as we went. All the time, we hoped we'd never reach that door. As we got closer and closer, we recited the Lord's Prayer. I turned the knob on the heavy oak door and, to our astonishment, the door opened all by itself. That door had never opened without a protest until then. It was scary. We began to panic and almost changed our minds. We could clearly distinguish between our different heartbeats – we were that afraid. We tiptoed to her room. Aunt Rhonda was dressed like a bride with a white lace veil over her head. Her hands were crossed over her breasts and she was an ugly grey colour like someone had powdered her all over with ashes. Her eyes were sort of half closed and her legs had grey purple spots on them. We touched her on the count of three. She was ice cold, and Bobby decided she must be really dead. Lilly, Betty, and I didn't believe him. Bobby tried to pinch her but his nails broke off. We wanted more proof. So we called her name. She didn't answer."

As my memory took me back, my body crawled with disgust at what we had done. "Ohhhh…" I cried. How I wanted to kick myself.

Why was I not born without a sense of right and wrong? I wondered. Why could I not just have forgotten this awful thing instead of spending years torturing myself with guilt?

"Go on, Savannah," Uncle Daniel insisted.

"Ohooooh... fiddlesticks..." I said, at the point of panic now. "OK... here goes. I pulled the bamboo pole with the ropes through the window. Then we all helped to tie her down to her bed. She was rigid, but we managed. With the bamboo pole in hand, we took turns beating the old bat! Bobby hit her with all his strength, and her corpse broke wind! We froze again thinking she wasn't dead after all and was going to grab the bamboo pole and beat the crap out of us. Uncle Daniel, do dead people break wind?" I asked, still looking at Ruby's pretty face.

There was no answer for, as Grandma would say, "all hell broke loose" around me. Uncle Daniel and Bobby rolled like unhinged lunatics on the kitchen floor, their bodies contorted with laughter. "Bobby swiped her with the bamboo pole and her long white dress flipped up! We panicked and threw handfuls of pebbles and dirt at her. We hastily shoved some pebbles up her nose and into her earholes. Bobby called Betty a 'chicken' for something or another and they started to fight. Lilly and I were too afraid. We could hardly part them. They stopped fighting when Betty bit Bobby on the head. We abandoned the bamboo pole on top of her and raced from the room in fright. We ran all the way back to Peaceful View, hid in the summer house, and waited to be found out."

I sighed. Finally, my guilt was laid down. Relieved, I sat light-headed still studying Ruby's pretty face.

Uncle Daniel managed to pull himself together.

"Savannah, are you alright?" he asked.

"Yes, I am alright now my confession is over with. One more nightmare behind me. The old mare will stop tormenting my sleep now."

Though this appalling episode may never leave my memory, I had finally talked about it. I stood up and walked out of the kitchen. My destination now was the bathroom and that much-needed bath, and some me time. I was going to scrub Aunt Rhonda out of my system.

******

I stood surveying myself in front of the floor-to-ceiling mirror in the bathroom. I wasn't sure exactly what I was hoping to find except, perhaps, my own reflection looking back at me. Nevertheless, I no longer felt so utterly guilty nor was I afraid and lonely anymore. I was not sure about Bobby, but being with him and Uncle Daniel gave me a sense of belonging once more. I twirled around, caught the hem of my skirt, and lifted it to my face. I peered at myself from behind my makeshift mask. I hadn't realised my skirt was so utterly transparent. Standing there, I could see right through to my skin. I frowned and began dancing about to imaginary music in my head. It seemed I had shed the gloom of Aunt Rhonda and was finally liberated from my guilty secret. I unbuttoned my blouse and let it slide over my shoulders; then I shrugged and it slipped quietly to the floor. I pulled the drawstrings on my gipsy skirt and, it too, floated down my legs like a deflated parachute. Both ended up in a pile around my feet. Like a woman without a care in the world, I carelessly kicked them aside.

I had stopped hankering after those extra inches a long time ago and had grown to accept my petite size. My midriff needed a little attention, but I had six months of leisurely sunshine hours to work on it. I was a woman in tune with my body and would notice the slightest changes in my shape. I was conscious of the few extra inches I had gained over the last few months. I turned to look at my bum with appreciation and sincere thanks to my Creator. In spite of all that had happened in my life, I had much to be thankful for. I was perfect in neither body nor mind, but, compared to others less fortunate, I was truly blessed. I smiled at my reflection, sat down on the floor, and pulled my rucksack closer to me.

"Now, let's see what I need. Mmm… my favourite scented candles."

I ran one of the candles languidly under my nose, inhaling the uplifting fragrance of lavender. Then there were the oils too. I placed my little personal stereo on top of the vanity unit behind the bathroom door and popped in a disc. In a little while, music just loud enough for my ears, would ooze out to finish the calm feeling settling over me. This was my personal moment. My "me time" – deliberate and totally selfish. I could indulge my mind and body and be immersed by the possessive feel of hot fragrant water. There was soft music and scented candle lights to carry my mind on a journey that would follow no particular route but just drift effortlessly in search of all things beautiful. I wasn't going to think of anything that would upset my equilibrium. My mind would follow its own path without any interference from my perfidious heart or me.

"Mmm… bliss," I sighed. "Now, what else do I need? Oh yes! A lighter for the candles and bubbles too."

I flipped the top of the lighter that belonged to Martin, and the candles flickered into life. I pressed play on the stereo, and music transformed the bathroom into an oasis of calm. Then I went and spoiled it all by looking down at my feet! I closed my eyes in depression. I hated my feet. My love of high heels during my self-conscious teenage years had taken its toll. I had two award-winning bunions, which spoiled my tiny feet.

"I must do something about my feet," I said, groaning. The sight of Samson and Delilah depressed me. To spare myself, I climbed into the bath and slid down beneath the foamy bubbles of lavender. I came up for air from time to time and then dived under the water again. I alternated between exfoliating my skin with far too much verve and disappearing under the water. Finally, it was time to turn the shower on for a thorough rinse. I pulled the plug, and the water began its descent with a noisy chorus of gurgles and sucking sounds. There was a knock on the door, and I jerked my head out from under the shower. I was thoroughly annoyed at the infringement on the only time I had had to myself so far. I gulped on the air before answering.

"Gordon Bennett," I grumbled grudgingly under my breath, "I can't even have a bath in peace,"

"Yes, what is it?" I asked.

"Hey… it's me, Bobby. You alright in there?"

"No. I'm not alright. I've just hanged myself from the shower rail," I answered with mockery.

To be honest, I could have cried, for I was thoroughly enjoying my bath and needed this time to unwind and recharge my batteries. Cheesed off with this invasion, I wanted to punch Bobby through the locked door. In fact, I felt like shattering every window in the house with an ear-splitting scream, but I wasn't Ella Fitzgerald. In the back of my mind, my doubt returned. I hadn't planned on dwelling on it, but the knock at the door changed all that. If only - I could say the words racing through my head, but I was trying to be a good Christian, and, anyway, my conscience would only plague me afterwards.

"No need to bite my head off. I just wanted to know you are OK."

Bobby sounded amused at my annoyance.

"Bearing in mind we're in the same place, what do you suppose could have happened to me, Bobby?"

I grabbed my loofah and began to scrub myself again.

"Jeeez, you really are pissed off," Bobby laughed.

I suppressed my irritation at his thoughtlessness. I clenched my teeth together tightly and snarled at him through the door.

"As it goes, I am cheesed off. I need some space. Time to think. To be alone. I'd like to have had my bath in peace. It's not much to ask, Bobby."

"I didn't mean to upset you. You just got up and walked out of the kitchen. I was concerned. Savannah, you and I have to talk. You know what I mean?" Bobby whispered through the door.

"No, Bobby. I don't know what you mean, but I have a feeling you are going to tell me."

He hesitated, drumming his fingers on the door.

Then he whispered again, "We know Claude is around here somewhere. But we will find him."

I didn't answer. Instead, I found myself wondering again whether Bobby was trying to frighten me and, make her run away and hide in a dark silent place like I used to do as a child. The enjoyment of my planned leisurely bath seeped away like murky water running down a drain.

If I had put the threat to my life at the back of my mind, Bobby brought it back to the fore again. As a little girl, I had suffered at Uncle Claude's hands and knew he was capable of carrying out his threat. Now he had added ammunition to fuel his hate-filled heart. He was ready to ignite his dormant flames of hate once more. Suddenly I knew I wasn't going to run away from this threat any more than I was prepared to lie down and die.

"Savannah, try not to worry. We are looking for him... we'll find him."

Shedding Aunt Rhonda's ghost earlier had strengthened me. Now it appeared I had only lulled myself into a false sense of security. My whole life had been based on doubt, half truths, guilt, and fear of the human race, but I was done with that now. I stepped out of the bath and picked up a towel.

"I will tell you this for nothing, Bobby. I will fight him all the way. I am not the frightened abandoned child he used to torture. I won't be running for the airport clutching my passport. I'm here to stay."

As I dried myself, I wondered why some humans were so utterly contemptible. My doubt about Bobby had staggered me somewhat at first, for he and I were very close as children. Yet, I could not afford to dismiss my doubt. My face contorted as I calmly evaluated the situation. I decided to probe a little bit.

"Bobby, whose idea was it to put me in Aunt Eva's bedroom?"

"You loved the mountains, Savannah. That room has the best view. Why do you ask?"

"You've not answered my question, Bobby."

"Savannah, there was nothing sinister in my mind when I suggested Aunt Eva's room."

"Yeah… I bet. I knew it was your idea. It had to be."

Bobby became quiet, giving nothing back in his own defence. I ventured further.

"Just in case you have anything else up your sleeve, I'm one step ahead of you."

"That sounds ominous, Savannah."

"Not really, Bobby. It depends how you interpret it. That's all."

"Are you still pissed off with me for interrupting your bath?"

"No – not anymore. Why do you ask?"

"Just making sure what I can hear in your voice is real."

"And what can you hear in my voice, Bobby?"

"You sound less uptight. Know what I mean?"

"I am a bit selfish about my personal space. I can be solitary at times too. I hope you will understand that."

"Yeah, I do. I won't be invading your personal space in a hurry again. Sorry about that."

"At least we understand each other on that score now."

"Yeah, we do… yeah."

"Good. Now will you do me a favour please, Bobby?"

"Just say the word, Savannah. I'm at your service."

I decided to let the "at your service" pass. I knew it was a dig and that it had everything to do with our grandmother's will. Bobby had said I had been left "everything" during our conversation in the summer house. But I wasn't going to think about that for the moment. I would return to it at a more opportune time.

"The boxes in Aunt Eva's room… Be a sweetheart and help Uncle Daniel take them over to my bedroom, please."

"We carried them across a while ago. Don't tell me you didn't hear us struggling."

"Thank you. No, I didn't hear a thing."

Bobby's self assurance had returned. I was glad, for I had no wish to make him uncomfortable. I sensed there was something on Bobby's mind – something other than Claude and the death threat hanging over my head. It was a familiar itch that I knew wasn't going to go away until I had scratched it.

"Savannah… are you alright in there? Are you still there?"

I looked up at the window. It had started to rain again. My eyes followed a single droplet of water as it ran down the glass and disappeared. I began to wonder whether my grandmother had left the future of Peaceful View to me as a way of testing me from the grave!

"Savannah… answer me. Man, are you still there? Savannah?" Bobby hollered my name.

I thought I had better let him know I was still there and was alright.

"Yes Bobby, I'm alright. I just lapsed for a moment. I was watching the rain against the window – a bit lost in my thoughts."

"Geee… Savannah. Don't do that again, man. It's scary."

He actually sounded concerned, but I wasn't going to be fooled. I would keep my eyes on Bobby's every move.

"Bobby, go to my room. We can continue talking there."

I finished drying myself and pulled on a cotton caftan I had bought in Egypt a year ago. I opened the door and walked through to my bedroom.

Bobby wasn't in the room so I looked outside the door to see if he had arrived and was waiting there. He wasn't there. I settled myself on the window seat, and presently, there was a knock on the door.

"It's open, Bobby. Come on in."

He breezed in and handed me a small plate of thickly-cut sandwiches of sardines and cucumber.

"Uncle D says you are to eat them all. You can't leave a crumb."

I was starving and dived straight into the sandwiches without offering Bobby any.

"I am so hungry, I wouldn't get too close if I were you, for I might just take a bite out of you too!"

We laughed together, and Bobby sat down on the bed.

"You know, Savannah, everything about you reminds me of Grandma."

Bobby said this loosely as if he'd borrowed the thought from someone else.

"If I reflect any of Grandma's qualities, then I'm honoured. She stood for the things that are important to me. I have strived to emulate her. If I reflect just one of her qualities, I have achieved a small part of my goal in life." I decided it was going to be now or never. I had to scratch that itch. "Bobby, I sense there might be something on your mind. Do you want to talk to me about anything – anything worrying you?"

"What makes you think I have something on my mind?" Bobby asked, without making eye contact.

With his elbows supporting his weight, he leaned back on the bed.

"It's just a feeling. I can always tell when someone is holding out on me. I've been there a number of times; the signs aren't hard to spot."

"Truth is, there is something... but it can wait."

I knew it. That inner voice had told me, "This is the way – walk in it." This voice never fails me when I listen to it.

"I'd like to hear it now, Bobby. You've ruined my bath because of this very thing. Let's hear it."

I waited for him to speak.

"Well... I was wondering if you would let me choose a few acres of land here at Peaceful View. The old girl left me some money, and I have saved a bit of my own. I want to build a little ranch – something I can call mine."

Although I knew Bobby meant no disrespect by referring to Grandma as "the old girl", I didn't like it at all. I would have to say something about it to him, but not now. Right now, I was only concerned with what was on his mind.

"I think you are being a bit selfish. Let's face it, Bobby. This is not the time to be thinking about your share of Peaceful View, is it?"

"That's exactly why I would have waited. I had a feeling you'd be annoyed."

Though Bobby's timing wasn't exactly spot on, and his request seemed calculating too, I smiled at him nonetheless. Regardless of whether my suspicions about him were right or wrong, what he was asking for was his right. The timing was way off, but why should he put his life on hold to suit me? I argued in my mind.

"Bobby... what I don't understand is why you are asking me to give you land you already have. Are you asking for an additional amount?"

"I don't understand, Savannah."

"What don't you understand, Bobby?"

"Additional land – what do you mean?"

He gestured with opened palms just like Grandma used to do. The memory softened my fickle heart and I gave in.

"Do you remember showing Grandma a section of land you wanted as a boy?"

"Yes, I remember. But did the old girl remember?"

"Whether or not she had remembered, the land is yours, Bobby."

"I would be really grateful if that is the case, Savannah."

"No need to be grateful. It's true. It's your birthright. Grandma's letter says, if I am agreeable, you are to have five acres of land. Didn't you know that, Bobby?"

"No, I didn't. Uncle D said he wouldn't discuss anything until you came home."

"I am giving you twenty acres, however. I hope that will be enough for you, Bobby?"

He beamed, and I could see he was both pleased and surprised.

Why he had thought I would rob him of what was rightfully his troubled me. Something else troubled my mind too – Bobby's timing. Why was he not prepared to wait at least until after Uncle Daniel had spoken to me? Why was he in such a hurry to get his hands on his share of the land? There was only one way to find out.

"Bobby, tell me, have you any idea how soon Claude plans to end my life?"

CHAPTER 12

I picked up a bottle of moisturising oil and began rubbing it into my skin. Bobby sat on the bed, rigid, mouth wide open, staring at the bedroom door. He was transfixed as if struck by a thunderbolt. I wondered whether some unseen being only he could see had entered the room. If I didn't know better, I would say Bobby had arrived from another time, had taken a deep breath, and forgotten to breathe out again. I glanced at him for the third time, and then decided to try and bring him back from whatever world he was lost in.

"Bobby… you're catching flies. Your mouth is wide open."

Getting no response, I gave up, leaving him to his own devices. The goings-on since returning to the island left little to be desired at that moment. The dreams I had nurtured of Peaceful View had become like a noose around my neck. My present existence and the unstable situation, which I could neither control nor predict, made me feel sorry for myself. If it wasn't for my ability to vanish into other worlds, I could have gone insane.

"I don't know how to answer your question, Savannah. I don't understand the question." Bobby had finally woken up from his dream world!

"What question is that, Bobby?" I asked.

I had moved on and wasn't expecting him to answer me.

"The one you asked… a-ab-about death!"

"I thought maybe you're in contact with Claude… and you might have an idea."

Given no one except Ken knew I would be coming home, my question and train of thought appeared somewhat off the radar. However, as it had been known, Claude had threatened to kill me the day I returned there. My question stood to reason. It was inevitable. I would have returned home sooner rather than later to sort out our grandmother's affairs.

"Never mind, Bobby. All will be revealed. I dare say, it'll come out in the wash."

"Gee… thank you, Savannah… thank you."

"What are you thanking me for, Bobby?" I asked, uncertain.

Surely, he could not be thanking me for asking him the time and date of my impending execution! Scarcely daring to breathe, for I didn't want to miss a single word Bobby might have to say, I looked to him for clarity.

"For the land… the twenty acres…"

Strange, I thought. We appeared to be at cross purposes. I had the notion we were talking about the threat to my life.

Bearing that in mind, I replied with some annoyance now, "Don't thank me, Bobby. Thank your dead grandmother. She left it to you."

"Grandma left everything at your disposal, Savannah. If you had disagreed… that would have been it," Bobby said.

For the umpteenth time my conversations with Bobby got tedious. I couldn't help thinking; Bobby was either out to confuse me or to drive me away from Peaceful View.

"Bobby, you selected that land as a boy. Grandma wanted you to have your wish. Did you actually believe I would deny you what is your birthright?" Bobby couldn't answer me. So I answered for him, "I wouldn't have, Bobby. I wouldn't have gone against Grandma's wishes, and I certainly had no intention of denying you, your right."

I speculated that if the situation had been reversed, my cousin might not have been as generous to me as I was to him. Bobby and I had grown into two different individuals. Each had our own morals. As children, we were inseparable. But the years spent living apart in different parts of the world, had created two very different people. We hadn't seen or spoken to each other in over twenty years. People change, and the harsh lessons I had been learning since arriving at Peaceful View forced me to see others for what they truly were: imperfect humans – prone to do the wrong things as opposed to the right ones. Ordinarily, I would never have harboured thoughts of Bobby's involvement with Claude. But the unnatural situation on Peaceful View opened up all kinds of possibilities in my mind. It seemed to me; evil sat below the veneer of every situation I'd encountered since arriving home. Adam and Eve had a lot to answer for, I thought to myself.

"Savannah, I wasn't sure what you would do. I'd hoped you would have honoured Grandma's promise to me… and you have. I'm really touched."

Bobby turned towards me, his long eyelashes swept up, and I saw something in his eyes. My body reacted, and, as if to hold him off, I held my hands, palms up, towards him.

"We are different people, Bobby… you and me. Neither of us knows each other anymore. That's evident, because we both have doubts about each other," I said calmly.

"Oh," said Bobby, sounding put out by my remark.

"I have doubts about you, and you have doubts about me," I explained and got up from the window seat.

I'd had enough of this conversation and enough of the uncertainty that surrounded me. It was time to dry my hair and get dressed. I hadn't seen Uncle Daniel for hours, and I wondered whether he was hiding from me. I wrapped my hair in a towel and began going through my belongings to find something to put on. I hadn't eaten anything substantial since stopping on the way to Peaceful View and that was yesterday. I was positively ravenous now, and my tummy was groaning in protest.

"I can't think why you'd doubt me, Savannah. You want to talk about it?"

"Not right now, Bobby. Some other time. Tomorrow perhaps?" Bobby nodded, and I was relieved he had no plans to pursue the subject. I wanted desperately to talk to Uncle Daniel about my worrying thoughts. I walked to the door and held it open. "I need to get dressed now, Bobby."

He jumped off the bed and walked towards the open door without hesitation, but then he stopped. He took my hands in his and looked intently into my face.

"Savannah…I don't know what you have on your mind. But I want you to know I will never do a single thing to harm you."

"Thanks, Bobby. Now I must get dressed. I am starving," I said with a smile.

"OK… I'll go help Uncle D. He must be wondering what's taking us this long."

"I doubt that. If he was concerned, he'd have come to find us," I said.

I was more than a little wound up about my uncle's absence. It occurred to me, Uncle Daniel had deliberately made himself scarce.

"He knows we are together, Savannah. He's just giving us time to catch up."

"I guess you are right. Now scoot. See you in a while."

I pushed him gently out the door and locked it behind him. I needed a little while on my own to gather my thoughts. I returned to the window seat and picked up the massage oils again.

The soothing strokes of my hands soon deflected my thoughts to my personal needs – the need I harboured of belonging to a husband who would be sincere, loving, and having the qualities of an old-school gentleman of principle – one I could give my love to for the rest of my days. I thought of my longing for a place where I would feel safe and where I felt I belonged – a home where my natural desires could be fulfilled and my creative abilities executed to perfection. There was so much love inside of me – it literally cried out to be released. I sat preening myself as if preparing for that special person. Yet I knew in my heart that the husband of my dreams did not exist and probably never would. I had a habit of trusting the wrong people and wasn't prepared to gather up the broken pieces of my heart again. Soon my mood and thought malfunctioned, and I was pulled back to another memory from my past. My head came down, and I rested my chin on my knees. A lump had grown in my throat and was threatening to end my life before Claude got the chance.

Memories of Claude.

My eyes followed the landscape across the meadow, and then down into the pastures. I was eight years old and was a confident rider. My favourite horse was Grandma's mare Jennie. I had just mounted her after tying her to the dogwood tree. I was going to meet Bobby for a race across the edge of the pastures. As I rode along singing happily in between talking to Jennie, I came upon Claude lying on his back under the shade of some trees. He leapt to his feet in front of Jennie, frightening the usually docile horse. Jennie bolted, throwing me several feet into the air. I landed in thick thorny bushes and screamed in agony. Claude walked towards me, and my childish heart hoped he would pick me up and take me home. But he left me lying there injured while he ran after Jennie. After securing the horse to a tree, he returned and stood towering over me laughing.

"You little shit. I was hoping you'd broken your neck... or even maybe died!" he said, laughing even harder than before.

Then he dragged me from the bushes by my legs and lay me in the heat of the burning sun. He unzipped his trousers and turned me into a human urinal – he urinated over me. I remember closing my eyes tightly so I wouldn't see. Everything had turned black - I passed out. I bit on my lip now to hold back the pain that always accompanies memories of Claude. I threw my head back to prevent my tears from falling – I stayed this way for a while. I shook my head now, as if to put the memory back in the secret part in my heart. Then, mercifully, I heard approaching footsteps and the memory dissolved.

"Savannah, you still aren't dressed, princess?" Uncle Daniel said with a measure of dismay as he stepped into the room.

"I'm... No – not yet. It won't take me a minute. Is dinner ready? I'm so hungry."

"Savannah, we are having company this evening. I hope you won't mind, princess."

I turned away from him. I didn't want to spoil his plans for the evening, and the sight of him tugged on my heartstrings. But the last thing I wanted was company.

"I do mind. I didn't want to see anyone – and certainly not that girlfriend of yours. She is the last person I want to see. I can't stand her."

Straight away, I regretted my words. I have never denied my uncle anything within my powers. While I disliked this woman and planned to see her off the scene, I would not have dealt with it this way. I felt guilty now. Why the words flew out when Ellen wasn't even in my thoughts, I don't know.

"Savannah, we can talk about Ellen later on. Tonight is planned already. What do you want me to do?"

"I told you. I don't want to see anyone – not just yet. I wanted us to spend the evening together… just you and me. I need to talk to you, Uncle Daniel – alone:"

Looking into his face, I saw the bruises I had put there. In addition, I saw something that reminded me of parts of my childhood - something I have never reconciled myself to. Uncle Daniel looked very ill – seriously ill. On top of it all, fatigue was etched in every painful line on his face. I didn't want to accept what was so clearly there, but it was useless denying what I saw.

He must have mistaken the look on my face for stubbornness, for he said, "Alright, Savannah. It's a bit late, mind. But if that's what you want… it's done:"

His eyes now searched mine and he waited for my reaction. I crumbled, and my resolve came crashing down around me.

"No – don't cancel. Whatever you have planned is… OK with me. We have time to spend together later on."

"Thank you, princess. It will be worth it, you'll see."

I nodded my head in defeat.

"We must talk soon, Uncle Daniel. I don't want anyone else around – just you and me:"

"How about tomorrow? We'll take a drive away from Peaceful View. We'll go to the beach and spend the day there. Do you still love fish, Savannah?"

"Do I still love fish? I positively adore the stuff. I have a love affair with fish."

We both laughed.

"Then I know just the place. Little Ochi -, it's in Alligator Pond."

"It's a date I'm looking forward to already. The fish, that is, not the alligator!" I quickly added, making light of my disappointment.

The frail appearance of my uncle made me want to trade places with him, to make his life all right for him again. In addition to what I'd done to him, his once handsome face showed years of alcohol abuse. I wondered if he believed I had no idea of his alcoholism. I was sure my coming home had added further worry to his already worn-out shoulders. My mind questioned whether I would be able to help him quit the habit. I had six months to try and vowed in my heart to expend all my efforts on my uncle. I loved him enough to devote every second of my time to him.

"Alright, Savannah. Get yourself prettified , and then come and help me prepare for our guests," he said firmly, and followed with a stiff nod of his head.

"Uncle Daniel, you've not told me who's coming to dinner. Anyone I know?"

"Oh… my head is not what it used to be." He scratched his now neatly-trimmed hair to bring the point home. "I forgot to show you a new set of rooms I prepared for you. Come, let me take you there. I will reveal our guest's identity on the way."

My uncle's little secret tickled me. I began to deliberate who might be coming. Really, I didn't care who came to dinner anymore. I would do almost anything to take away the burden he carried on his exhausted shoulders. I linked my arm into his and followed him back to the corridor where Aunt Eva's room was. I hesitated as we approached the door.

"No… it's not Aunt Eva's room, Savannah."

He made a ghoulish face at me, and I hid my face behind my hands in mock fright!

"You're in the guest bedroom. It's on the other side of the house. Come."

He took my hand, and I tagged along through the dining room, an unfurnished room, then onto another corridor. This newly discovered corridor ran behind the bedroom I had used earlier. A door sealed this area off from the rest of the house. I would never have guessed it was there. The additional rooms were almost secret and very private. Aunt Eva's house was turning out to be an Aladdin's cave. I was sure I wasn't going to find my way around. The design of the house was clearly not accidental. It was so cleverly executed; I suspected Uncle Arnold was responsible for its uniqueness. Uncle Daniel produced a set of keys from his pocket. He opened one of three doors along the corridor and ushered me into a refreshingly beautiful and spacious sitting room. He opened another door leading off the sitting room, and waved me in.

"Your favourite colour, Savannah – is it still blue or is it lavender?" Uncle Daniel asked.

I nodded, for I was distracted by the love I saw in my uncle's weary eyes. I could have reached up and took hold of it. I lifted his arms and placed them around me; he encircled me into them.

"Do you know how much I love you, Uncle Daniel?"

"Yes I do. But tell me, Savannah, why is it you don't call me Papa anymore?"

"Ooo… I don't know. I guess it's called… growing up."

A sudden feeling of guilt began to crawl over my mind. I dismissed the feeling for I was certain that guilt would return to visit me another day. I unloosened Uncle Daniel's arms from around me and stepped away. I looked more closely at the beautiful rooms and their restful shades of blue.

"In answer to your question… I still love both colours."

It seemed to have just dawned on my uncle that I was actually there in the flesh with him. His eyes surveyed me, and my heart wanted to take on whatever pains he bore. For years he had been pleading with me to come home but I was afraid – afraid of the memories I refused to confront and afraid I wouldn't live up to my grandmother's expectations. I was here now and, with God's guidance, I aimed to do everything in my powers to make things right for all concerned, especially my uncle. I simply couldn't afford to litter my thoughts with Claude, Bobby, or fear anymore. My uncle needed me, and I had procrastinated long enough. I wondered, though, whether my homecoming was too late.

"Savannah… what's the matter? You are scolding."

Instead of answering, I leaned my head to one side and smiled for him.

"That's a little better. It didn't reach your eyes, though!"

I took his arm again, spun him around, and followed this up by dancing around the room. I finished off with a curtsy in front of him. Uncle Daniel threw his head back and really laughed – we both laughed. For a moment, it felt like the old days.

"Savannah, I am so happy to have you back. I am here for you. Never forget that."

Uncle Daniel's love had been unfaltering. I had been his little girl, and he had been my doting papa; he gave me both love and attention. He never lost his patience with me during those turbulent years when I would disappear into a world of my own. When I hid away in the hills for days on end, he never scolded me. Instead, he would tenderly try to find the reason for my disappearance. He never thought I was bad or obstinate, neither did he forced me to do anything I didn't want to do. When the rest of the family thought I had lost my mind – because Pastor Mac said so – he thought I was just enquiring and unique.

"Oh, Uncle Daniel… have we got time? Will I be able to make it alright for you?"

I fell to my knees clutching at his leg.

I was so afraid my time with him was going to be cut short.

"Savannah… what is it? What's wrong, princess?"

The worried look on my uncle's face soon forced me to collect up my senses. I pulled myself together and got to my feet.

"Don't mind me. I'm just a mushy fool. I've stayed away too long, that's all."

"You are here now… that is all that matters," said my adoring uncle.

I vowed to keep my fears under wraps from here on.

"Alright. I will need my things brought here. I'll get dressed and come and help you," I said as cheerfully as I could.

"Right. I'll go and get that organised for you. You'll be safe here!"

"Safe? That's an odd thing to say."

"I am going to be next door to you. Robin will be staying a few days. I've put him… on the other side of you – I mean your room is between us both."

"Robin? Who is that? A bird? Does he have a red breast?" I giggled, and then skipped around the room like a child with a new toy.

"Now, now, Savannah. I don't think Robin will find that amusing."

He raised his brow at me and I mimicked him raising mine.

"He might have a sense of humour, Uncle Daniel." I paused, and then I added, "No… I guess not. Bobby did say Mr Stein might come by. I remember Mr Stein. But… Robin? No."

I caught myself just in time. I had given Bobby my word in the summer house that I'd say nothing of what he had told me. Now, I had told Uncle Daniel I knew about Mr Stein's visit. I prayed he wouldn't question me for I would not be able to tell him a lie.

"Doctor Pitter's son. He is older than you. He went to study law in England some years before you left."

"Oh… yes. I vaguely remember pictures of the adored only child on the walls at the Pitter's house."

I failed to say I was awfully jealous of Robin as a child; I had wanted his parents to be the ones I didn't have.

"He is our guest this evening. So is Gus and Dr Pitter."

"Wow! Dr Pitter? Is he still alive?"

I grew excited at the thought of seeing Dr Pitter again. How absolutely marvellous, I thought. Now I couldn't wait. Dr Pitter and Mr Stein! Just seeing them both was enough to guarantee a splendid evening.

"Very much so. But, like the rest of us, he is getting on a little now."

"I should think so. He must be going on eighty… or somewhere around there."

"Now, princess, let your old uncle go and finish dinner."

Uncle Daniel placed his hands on my shoulders and kissed me on the head.

"I'll get dress in the bedroom you took me from. That way, I'll waste no more precious time. How about that?"

He stretched out a hand and I took hold of it.

"See you in a while then," said Uncle Daniel.

I blew him a kiss and began combing my tangled hair.

CHAPTER 13

Uncle Daniel was bent over the sideboard collecting up cutlery, when I walked into the dining room. He looked up and smiled broadly. I spun around so he could see my transformation. I ran my hands over my dress and fluttered my eyelashes at him. I wanted to see if he approved of the woman his little girl had grown into. He put down the cutlery and took slow careful steps towards me. I watched with delight as his careworn features gradually softened. As he drew closer, a look of surprise settled over his face and then spread into a pleasing smile. As he turned his head this way then that, his broad smile drew attention to the single dimple he had inherited from Grandma. For the first time, I saw a striking resemblance between mother and son. I had never noticed this before; it gave me Goosebumps and a feeling of déjà vu.

"M-my princess. you look beautiful."

"You are so complimentary, Uncle Daniel. Keep up the flattery. I might get to like it." I giggled and twirled around for him.

"I'm not flattering you, princess. I'm looking at a stunning young woman."

I took comfort in the pride I saw in my uncle's eyes. I was glad I had turned out reasonably well adjusted and didn't have a tree growing out of my face or something. Pastor Mac had rendered me "the devil's child" and had painted a very bleak picture of my future – all because I had set the vestry on fire and tried to dig up my dead Aunt Vicky. I am sure, like the rest of my family, my uncle must have wondered what would become of me on the morning I had waved a tearful goodbye to them all. I was on my way to the airport and was leaving my beloved home and family behind.

"Oh, rubbish! You are biased, and you're embarrassing me now."

I rocked back and forth on my heels.

"Does the truth embarrass you, Savannah?"

He looked tenderly at me, but I wasn't going to elaborate. Hopefully we would discover each other all over again as the days went by.

"Yes…some truths do," I answered, as I walked over and took his arm.

"This is the last meal you are going to cook. From tomorrow I'll do the cooking. You are going to take it easy, you hear?"

I poked him gently in the ribs and felt nothing but bones.

"Yes, ma'am. I hear you loud and clear."

I took the tray of cutlery from him and went to the dining table. I set about getting the table ready for dinner. I tried to recall the last time when I had eaten a meal in Aunt Eva's house. I could hear voices down the hall - in fact I could hear several male voices. I listened and heard Bobby's voice in conversation but could not make out the others. I ignored the voices and continued setting out cutlery and crockery on the table. Uncle Daniel was busy around the stove, so I left him to cook his last meal in peace. When I had finished laying the table, I stepped back to look at my handiwork, but something was missing. Umm… flowers, I thought. On top of the sideboard was a vase of fresh flowers. I took a single bloom and placed it in a small vase, which I put in the centre of the dining table. "Yes. That's it. All we need now is food and bodies," I said to myself. Happy the table looked perfect, I walked to the window to ogle the stars.

Clouds swirled this way and that - then they merged together again and morph into ships, houses, strange-looking creatures, people, and animals. All was arrayed in gunmetal grey; I could not see a single star. The dark grey of the skies and the weird swirling of the clouds, lent a threatening feel to the heavens. Tonight, it seemed to be readying itself for something menacing. I could feel an element of warning in the rapidly-darkening clouds. A faint feeling of trepidation sent a tiny shiver through me. I dismissed the feeling and replaced it with my childhood days when I would lie on my back in the meadow and watch the clouds. I would stare up at the heavens enthralled and just watch the endless blue above. Fluffy cotton wool-like clouds hurried by, as if by appointment, to some distant place. Sometimes I saw what I had decided was the profile of a man who looked like Jesus Christ at the Passover supper. I walked away from the window.

"You're getting morbid," I said aloud.

I turned back and drew the curtains shut on the clouds and their disconcerting antics.

"Savannah… have you finished in there?" Uncle Daniel asked from the kitchen.

"Yes. I'm done. Do you want a hand in there?" I answered, as I heard footsteps approaching on the ceramic tiles in the hall. The door opened, and Bobby appeared in the doorway. He stood gawking at me.

"This is the second time today that I have seen you attempting to catch flies, Bobby. Pick up your jaws off the floor," I said, watching his expression.

"You've just knocked my socks right off my feet, Savannah. You look gooooood."

"Thank you, Bobby. You've scrubbed up well yourself."

He beamed his pearly whites at me, and then walked over.

"Table's set. Is dinner ready?" he asked, rubbing his hands together.

"I was about to go and help Uncle Daniel when you came in," I answered.

"Let's go and help him then."

Together we went into the kitchen where Uncle Daniel was putting the finishing touches to each serving dish.

"What can we do to help, Uncle D?" Bobby asked, tapping Uncle Daniel on the shoulder.

"I'm done here now. Let me wash my hands. Savannah, I'll introduce you to everyone and then we can eat."

I nodded. I wasn't sure whether it was the light or if it was due to the fact he had finally finished preparing dinner, but Uncle Daniel looked a little less stressed. It seemed he had been cooking all day, but I intended this to be his last. I would take over and ensure he got some rest. I was sure too that he needed to see a doctor. It didn't take a lot to work out that my darling uncle was very sick.

"Bobby, begin taking the food through to the dining room in ten minutes, OK?"

Bobby gave Uncle Daniel a salute in reply, and they clasped hands in some sort of private gesture.

"Kids – little boys trapped in men's bodies!" I said, as I playfully frowned at them. The two had a close relationship and I was pleased.

"Come, Savannah, let's go and get our guests. Bob, ten minutes," Uncle Daniel reminded Bobby.

We left the kitchen and walked out into the corridor and down the hall to the sitting room.

"Heaven's bells, Daniel. Who is this delightful young woman?"

Mr Stein charged towards me. I stifled a giggle for I would have recognised Mr Stein without any introduction. Apart from his now completely white hair, he had not changed one little bit.

"Gus, this is Savannah, my niece."

This was obviously Uncle Daniel showing off. He will forever see me as his little girl – the daughter he never fathered. This was his moment, and I wasn't going to spoil it for him. I would be the adored daughter for as long as my uncle lived. Mr Stein shook my hand and lent forward and I kissed his jowl cheek.

"She smells good enough to eat, Daniel," Mr Stein stated.

I didn't know where to put my face. He used to say the same things to Aunt Victoria whom he had loved. But, to Grandma's great disappointment, another of her daughter's married a man she believed unsuitable. Aunt Victoria's heart had belonged to the miserable old grouch, Albert. And the love-struck Mr Stein had been left broken-hearted. As it turned out, life had dealt Aunt Vicky another of its awful blows. She had made the most terrible mistake. Grandma had been right, for my favourite aunt was dreadfully unhappy in her marriage. Mr

Stein would have made her a much better husband, but, unfortunately, it was not to be.

Uncle Daniel led me to the most eternally handsome man I had ever set eyes on. He was absolutely exquisite – an enchantment to my eyes and a delight to my senses. All of a sudden, my heart fluctuated between level-headed reasoning and feelings that exploded through my body.

"Wow," I said, accepting his hand in greeting and gazing dreamlike into the most captivating pair of eyes. They were a beautiful shade of green, and had a touch of gold that reminded me of autumn leaves. I was mesmerised by the man and his eyes.

"Savannah, you remember Dr Pitter, don't you? This is Robin, Dr Pitter's son."

I took no notice. I was more concerned with my fluttering heart and the wonderfully crazy thoughts sauntering through my head. Then there were my legs too. I was sure they were not going to hold out, for they trembled so. Whilst these strange and wonderful feelings caused confusion between my body and my head, I positively loved it.

"How do you do… Miss Hanson?" the gorgeous Robin spoke.

His voice stimulated every kind of thought in my frazzled head. I wanted to sit down and quieten my trembling legs, but my hand wouldn't let go of his.

"Savannah, come and say hello to Dr Pitter."

I felt a pull on my arm and looked around. Uncle Daniel was trying to drag me away from Robin and over to his father, Dr Pitter.

"Savannah, my dear, what an absolute pleasure to see you again."

The now fading blue eyes of Dr Pitter smiled warmly down at me. I was still dazed by the sight of his son and smiled an interminable smile back at him. My legs still wobbled from my hand-shake with Robin. The after effects now caused me to stagger into Dr Pitter's arms.

Dr Pitter had been special to me when I was a child. He had a place in the part of my heart, where all my most treasured memories were kept. Only two people knew how to reach me and that was him and Uncle Daniel. They knew how to get me to talk about things that gave me nightmares or things that made me run away and hide in the hills. Bit by bit, they would extract every fear and every pain I had hidden in my young heart. In the end, I never could hide anything from either Dr Pitter or my uncle. I stepped back as fond memories flooded my mind – memories I will treasure until the day I too would fall asleep in death. I was so very thankful Dr Pitter was still alive. I looked forward to spending some time in his company.

"Savannah, it's time to go into dinner. Come," I heard Uncle Daniel say.

But I needed to do something. I needed to touch Dr Pitter again just to make sure I wasn't dreaming. It would be a gesture that said what I couldn't. I reached up and touched Dr Pitter's cheek ever so tenderly. I kissed his cheek in a gesture of thanks – thanks for being alive and thanks for producing such an exquisite son. Now I could turn to join Uncle Daniel. As I did so, I saw Bobby was there too. We filed out of the sitting room and went into dinner. My eyes caught Bobby's and he gave me a knowing look. I took it to mean he had witnessed my embarrassing reaction to the statuesque Robin Pitter! I grasped my uncle's hand and hurried us from the sitting room.

We arrived into the dining room to find Bobby had brought the serving dishes out ready for us to eat. We each collected our little soup bowls and headed for the tureen on top of the sideboard. Our guests were asked to help themselves first before Uncle Daniel, Bobby, and me tucked in. Uncle Daniel took my bowl and poured a ladle full of delicious-looking seafood soup into it. Balancing the bowl on a plate I walked carefully to the dining table. I waited for Uncle Daniel to arrive at the table before sitting down. I wanted to see where he would sit, before taking my place at the table. He sat down at the head of the table and I sat to his right. Then the object of my anxiety took the chair directly opposite mine to the left of Uncle Daniel. I wanted to slip quietly out of the room but my empty stomach compelled me to remain seated.

Doctor Pitter sat at the other end of the table opposite Uncle Daniel, and Bobby and Mr Stein sat on either sides of him. With bottoms on all six chairs, I waited for Uncle Daniel to bless the table by thanking God through prayer. As a child, Grandma would make sure prayers were said before we ate our meals. Giving thanks before a meal had been the eleventh commandment at Peaceful View.

"Savannah, my child, have I told you - you look delightful?"

"Yes… Mr Stein… you did. Thank you again."

Oh how I wished he hadn't drawn attention to me again. I had quite successfully done that already for all had watched my disgraceful drooling in silence. I bet Robin Pitter noted me down as a desperate woman. I cringed and refused to look in his direction. I focused my eyes entirely on my little bowl of rich sweet-smelling soup, which I couldn't wait to dive into with my spoon.

"You're gladness to an old man's eyes, child."

Mr Stein's happiness at seeing me again – not as the self-willed child he remembered but as a grown woman – was getting the better of him. He looked kindly at me, and I wondered what was going on in the old man's head! I prodded Uncle Daniel under the table and glanced at him for help.

"Uncle Daniel. I don't know about the rest of you."

I looked at Bobby, Dr Pitter, and Mr Stein in turn, deliberately avoiding Robin's eyes.

"I'm starving hungry. Will someone say grace so I can eat?"

I was getting fed up of waiting, was famished, and my tummy groaned like the hinges on Aunt Rhonda's front door. The sounds of chattering voices made me even hungrier. It seemed everyone but me was waiting for their soup to go cold.

Behind us mouth-watering dishes cooked by Uncle Daniel waited on gentle heat. How I managed to resist the smells wafting towards me, I will never know, for I was close to giving up on life. I could have eaten the entire tureen of soup and the main course too. Finally, Mr Stein grew eager to get tucked in. He looked from Uncle Daniel to me and then to Bobby.

"Any objections if I say grace before we begin to eat?" asked Mr Stein.

As if I cared who prayed as long as someone gave a sincere thanks! All I wanted to do was get some food inside me.

"No. None at all," I said hastily, not waiting for Uncle Daniel to reply.

Unwittingly, I made eye contact with Robin and he winked at me! I bowed my head speedily in my own private prayer.

With the formalities of prayers over, it was soup spoons at the ready, and we tucked into our soup. It was worth the agonising wait. The soup was cooked to perfection, and we showed our appreciation by emptying all six bowls in record time. The main course of lobster, huge prawns, and a selection of fish were cooked in a rich Creole-style sauce, and that too was bliss. Every delicious mouthful produced moans of pleasure around the table. Uncle Daniel had been an excellent cook during my childhood and had lost none of his skills. Having told him I would take over the cooking, I had a tall order to follow. Nonetheless, I had a few surprises of my own.

"Daniel, this is wonderful. I always did enjoy your food. You are soooo good," said the sweet-natured and lovable Dr Pitter, who umm'd and aha'd his way through two helpings. Cutlery clicked against china and conversations became sparse as we pandered to our palate. Uncle Daniel watched me polish off the succulent lobster and smiled indulgently..

"See, Savannah, I remember all your favourite foods."

I nodded my approval, too busy feeding my face to utter a word; anyway, he caught me with my mouth full.

"Yes, I noticed. Thank you. I had forgotten how wonderfully you cooked. It's a lovely meal, Uncle Daniel. Delicious from start to finish."

My darling uncle seemed to be taking delight and a great amount of satisfaction watching the food disappear from the table.

"Yes," echoed Robin. "Daniel is a superb cook. I'm quite useless myself. I make a mean scrambled-eggs breakfast, though."

At this, Bobby began playing footsy with me under the table. I dared not look at him. I knew exactly what he was thinking and I discreetly kicked him under the privacy of the tablecloth.

"Savannah!"

I looked up. The object of my internal distress called my name! He was waiting for a response from me, and so, it seemed, was everyone else. The clattering of cutlery had ground to a halt. I avoided everyone's eye, and instead looked straight past Robin. Ruby's photograph once again proved to be my savoir. I focused my gaze on Ruby's elfin face.

"Crumbs!" I said, and everyone laughed except me.

"I'm sorry. Did you say something… to me?" I asked, keeping my eyes on Ruby's face.

I was worried should our eyes meet full on again, I may demand he kiss me, and that wouldn't do.

"I asked, how long will you be staying with us."

I was forced to look at him, and he held my gaze until I showed signs of submission.

"Mmm… ," I said, for I had forgotten how long I intended to stay. "Erm… Oh… initially I'd come… for six months."

"Initially, Savannah? Do you care to elaborate a little?"

I hesitated, picked up a glass, and poured myself some red wine. I took a mouthful, savoured the taste, and then swallowed.

"I am not certain whether I will stay that long, though," I replied a little tongue-in-cheek.

I didn't want to answer questions about my stay until I had spoken to my uncle and was certain that Bobby's intentions were honourable. In truth, I was unwilling to say anymore. I popped a chunk of Uncle Daniel's pickled cucumber into my mouth and crunched slowly. I expected Robin's legal background would alert him that all wasn't well but it didn't and he persisted.

"Oh," said Robin.

I glared at him, for I believed Robin Pitter may well be toying with me and I took exception to this. I made no reply.

"Any particular reason why you may not stay as long as planned, Savannah?"

Aunt Eva's dining chairs and Robin's inquisition-like questioning were testing my tolerance to the limit. Couldn't he detect I wasn't willing to talk about my stay?

"Would you mind if I didn't answer your question at this time?" I said, as I got up from the table.

The only effect the handsome Robin Pitter was having on me right now was one of irritation.

"Uncle Daniel, are we having dessert?"

I decided to take control and create a diversion. I began clearing the table.

CHAPTER 14

Mr Stein quickly gobbled up the remaining morsels from his plate. When he had satisfied himself every last crumb had gone, he pushed the plate towards me with a contented smile on his charming face. There was no need for asking if he had enjoyed the meal; his beaming face and empty plate said it all. I thought the small amount of food left on his plate must have been cold for he along with Dr Pitter, Uncle Daniel, and Bobby had stopped eating to watch the exchanges between Robin and me. I wondered what they had made of the situation. Earlier, when I first met Robin, I had been far too captivated by him to notice that the attraction between us was mutual. Strangely though, instead of feeling thrilled by this discovery, my heart sensed danger. A little voice whispered in my head, "Give him a wide birth, Savannah."

I quickly gathered up the empty plates and cutlery from the table, took a trayful into the kitchen, and stacked them in the sink. I was about to go back to collect the glasses, when I turned around and ran straight into Robin.

"So… rree. I had no idea you were behind me," I said apologetically.

His standing so close behind me was clearly a pretty dense thing to do, though. I could have had something hot in my hand and one or both of us could have been scalded! "Savannah… it's really my fault. I ought to be saying sorry."

"Yes, you ought to be," I said shortly. "For one, never creep up on me again. And secondly, I clearly gave you the impression that I didn't want to divulge too much about my plans, and yet you continue to question me." I lost my train of thought temporarily and found myself looking into his face. I was pleasantly surprised to find I felt none of the heat that had very nearly set me alight earlier in the evening. I was annoyed with him, and this made me view him through angry eyes. That served to pour cold water on my perfidious heart. I had enough on my plate and had no intention of complicating my life further. To have taken too much notice of the foolishness my heart had entertained, would be folly. I was determined the delusion I had created between my heart, my head, and Robin Pitter was laid to rest. "Just because my crazy female hormones got the better of me… a-and I drooled like a schoolgirl!" I added and thumped the work surface in frustration.

Although the words I wanted to say was on the tip of my tongue, I just couldn't get them out as logically as I wanted.

"Will you accept my apology… Savannah?" he said earnestly.

I studied his face and saw sincerity there. My heart said, "Forgive him, Savannah", but my head said, "Not yet. Punish him just a little bit more". I dismissed the reasoning of my heart, and followed the thought in my head instead.

"I have reasons for not wanting to divulge too much at this time. A little tact on your part… would be appreciated."

I knew my voice sounded cold and hoped he wouldn't interpret it as rudeness for that was not my intention. If I was to trust him as my uncle advised, Robin would have to learn quickly to interpret my thoughts and moods without me having to draw him a map. I wanted him to understand my fragile position. I would explain my fears in due course. This was neither the time nor place, and I wasn't going to be forced into anything until I was ready.

"Savannah, we have a lot to discuss. Getting off on the wrong footing wasn't very wise. I apologise again."

Annoyed as I was with him, I would accept his apology graciously for I knew he was sincere and that I had made my point.

"Your apology... is accepted," I said.

He stretched out his hand to seal peace between us. I looked at his hand for sometime, before taking it into mine.

"Savannah, your reluctance to speak openly about your stay... wouldn't have anything to do with your cousin... would it?"

Finally, the penny had dropped, I thought. But I couldn't reply, for my hand was still imprisoned in his; he watched my face keenly. I looked down at my hand in his and he let go.

"As it goes, yes... it is. How did you know?" I asked.

It was my turn to watch his face, for this question gave me further food for thought. I had begun to think I may be judging Bobby too harshly too soon. However, it appeared Robin may well have reservations of his own.

"Bobby is rather impulsive but means well."

He was giving very little away and was leaving me to draw my own conclusions –umm.

With his arms folded, his body leaning against the other end of the work surface, and his long legs crossed one over the other, he looked at home. The easiness and degree of familiarity he emulated suggested he and I were not strangers. Yet, in a sense, we hardly knew each other. Robin had been schooled in England from the age of twelve. He used to return to his island home during school holidays. I vaguely remember seeing photographs of him on every wall in his parents' home. Other than that, my memory of him was vague. Since Grandma's death, however, we had been acquainted through correspondence and phone calls. During one of his visits back to England, we were supposed to meet, but I had begged off at the very last minute. At thirty-nine, he had both experience and wisdom on his side. I was yet to learn the ways of both men and the world, but what I lacked in wisdom, I made up for in discernment. It was abundantly clear; my earlier drooling had amused him. But I was nobody's fool. I knew very well when a man was toying with me.

"What do you mean by impulsive?" I asked, moving away so I could read his facial expressions more clearly.

"We have hours of discussions and boxes of papers to go through. Can we go somewhere?"

"What? Right now?"

I looked around as if searching for a quiet corner to suggest. I wanted to hear what his thoughts were where Bobby was concerned, for he had given me nothing except to say Bobby was impulsive.

"If you are up to it tonight, we can begin."

He grinned and his breathtaking smile lit up his autumn eyes like two kilns. My perfidious body reacted in response, which made me wish I could wring myself dry of all feelings. It would have given me great pleasure to do so. However, I kept my reaction and thoughts in check and held his gaze until the fires in his eyes subsided. If I had toyed with the thought, this man could be a danger. My body's reaction to his smile, confirmed it. I would have to be constantly on alert and register this warning in the part of my brain, which sometimes proves lackadaisical to good reasoning.

"No… not tonight. But soon. I promise."

After all, it wasn't a life-or-death necessity. It had waited all these years – a few more days wouldn't harm.

"Tomorrow…?"

This was more of a challenge than a question, and I felt like a rabbit caught digging up carrots in the middle of a farmer's field. I twitched my mouth and raised my eyebrows with all intention of saying no.

"Yes, that will be fine."

I nodded my head to put accent on the agreement, and then remembered I already had a date – with Uncle Daniel. He was more important than boxes of papers and legal mumbo jumbo. In addition, I wasn't ready to spend hours in discussions with Robin anymore than I was ready to go through my dead grandmother's papers. I had to get out of this one quickly.

"Oh… no. Tomorrow is out of the question. I already have a date," I said feebly.

Having agreed already, I felt a little erratic changing my mind in the same breath.

"What? So soon? You certainly work fast, young lady. You've only just got here."

Why

He was being facetious, but of course, I was going to ignore him.

"Yes. I have a date. It will take up my entire day. Perhaps we can meet in the evening… if I'm not too shattered," I added over my shoulder, as I sauntered out the door towards the dining room.

I was having a wrestling match with my heart and needed to put space between Robin Pitter and me.

"Uncle Daniel… are we having dessert?" I asked, arriving by my uncle's side.

"Yes, we are, Savannah."

Uncle Daniel got up from his chair and excused himself from the table. I followed him leaving the others to carry on their conversations. Looking back, I saw Robin was about to sit down at the table again. I did a double take, for he had swapped seats and was sitting down in the chair next to the one I had occupied during dinner. If Robin Pitter wanted to play games with me, he had better be in good shape, I mused to myself, for I was one step ahead of him.

"I see you and Robin are getting acquainted, Savannah. I'm pleased, for he has much to discuss with you."

Uncle Daniel was in a jovial mood, and his weathered face had mellowed somewhat. I stood on tiptoes to give him a peck on the scratches I had so skilfully carved down the side of his face.

"Oh…" I said, feigning ignorance.

"He is a man of integrity. You can trust him, Savannah."

My uncle said this so solemnly, he would have sold Robin to me, whether I trusted him or not.

"Uncle Daniel, you sound as if you are handing me RP's CV."

"R… P?"

I made a face at my uncle, and then puckered my lips.

"I've just decided to nickname him by his initials."

"Savannah, be serious, will you?"

I inhaled then exhaled in the same breath. It was my way of saying I was getting bored and had more important things to mull over.

"I just want you to know that you can put faith in him."

I considered the relevance of my uncle's words for a second. What was he trying to tell me? I wondered. What advice was he going to give me? I felt mischievousness coming on.

"Just as long as his advice is all you want me to put faith in," I teased.

Patricia Barnes

If my grandmother trusted Robin, I knew I could trust him implicitly. I had no qualms about that, and anyway, it wasn't his legal integrity that I was concerned with. My concerns were the sparks ricocheting between us!

"Really… Savannah. You are as incorrigible as ever."

I thought my uncle looked a bit taken aback. I couldn't understand why, for I am sure I did not say what was on my mind.

"Well, Uncle Dearest. Don't put temptation in my way." Before Uncle Daniel said another word, I added, "OK..I know I can trust him. And his being Dr Pitter's son, adds a brownie point on his score card."

I scooped up some mango jelly on a spoon and popped it into my mouth.

"Umm… that's delicious. Uncle Daniel… erm… is he married?"

"Is, who married, Savannah?"

"You know very well who. Mr… Integrity," I said, looking out the window and hoping the answer my uncle supplied would be a resounding no. For although I sensed my heart was in danger, I was full of contradictions.

"He is, Savannah," Uncle Daniel said matter-of-factly,

Although the answer was exactly what I expected, it triggered a sudden chain of events. A bubble burst somewhere inside of me. My stupid heart deflated, and I wanted to lie down and let the world pass me by. Why, I wondered, were the men I came across either married or searching for affairs? They were too young or too old or were uneducated and without a hope in this world - let alone the one to come. Then there were the ones you wouldn't bother to look at once, let alone a second time! And last but by no means least, there were the opportunists who fell instantly in love with me, because I had a British passport. In their minds, I had the keys to the golden gates of the British Empire – a guarantee for a UK visa! Maybe I should just lie down and let the world pass me by after all. At least I would be safe.

What made me defy the usual state of affairs and dare to imagine this man would perhaps be single and searching for the ideal wife, would remain a mystery to me. I ought to have seen it coming, for Robin was university-Educated and was a lawyer. He was from a wealthy family and had probably already made a fortune in his own right. He was witty, eloquent, and dashingly handsome. He bore no resemblance to the usual desperate forty something trying to hang on to his fading ego, and he didn't need a visa for his parents were British. Robin Pitter had a full set of teeth, his own hair, vitality; I didn't need proof his libido was functioning at full capacity. To say I had lost interest in the conversation with my uncle was an understatement. I began putting out the dessert bowls with urgency. The sooner dessert was over, the sooner I could escape to my room.

"The bowls are ready, Uncle Daniel. Let's get it over with," I said sarcastically, as I banished all thoughts of Mr Integrity out of my mind.

"As you wish, Savannah."

Uncle Daniel pushed the glass bowl with the jelly towards me.

"Just plain jelly? Nothing else?" I asked without much interest.

Uncle Daniel did not answerer. Instead, he placed a tub of ice cream by the jelly bowl. I looked up and caught him watching me like he was seeing me in a new light or something. I wondered if he thought me unpredictable.

"Savannah, Robin's marriage isn't a happy one."

Uncle Daniel said this like he was able to feel whatever sadness Robin might or might not be going through in his marriage. Having lost interest, I couldn't have cared less what marital misery he suffered. If he was unhappy, he would have done something to repair his marriage, or he would have set both his wife and himself free. It was that simple – if something cannot be repaired, get rid of it.

"I've lost interest, Uncle Daniel. And anyway, if his marriage was that unhappy, he'd do something about it."

I had no time for men who claimed they were either unhappy in their marriages or that their wives didn't understand them. Then there were the pathetic lot who claimed they had an open marriage. To my mind, there were three types of men in this world: men of integrity – boys trapped in men's bodies, and those that stood no chance at all. I had no interest which category Robin fitted into.

"It's never that easy, Savannah," Uncle Daniel said.

His words left me speculating how on earth he would know anything about marriage, when he had never married himself.

"Yeah… whatever," I said with disdain, using the age-old cliché often used by the greater majority of the species called men.

In simple terms, it was called, "having your cake and eating it too." If I had my way; I'd probably have the majority of them dispatched to Siberia on a one-way ticket. I knew, for definite, there were decent men out there. But they were either past their sell-by date, or already happily married, or dead.

I picked up the tray with the dessert and headed back into the dining room. I placed it on top of the sideboard, and then began taking the bowls, two by two, to the table. I left mine on the tray. If Robin thought that by changing seats I would be sitting that close to him, he had another thing coming. I started at the top end of the table and placed Dr Pitter's bowl in front of him. He stroked my hand and nodded his thanks. Next it was Mr Stein, and then Uncle Daniel, Robin, and Bobby. Once I had finished serving dessert, I picked up my bowl and went into the kitchen. As a means of escaping to my room, I planned to draw on the depressed feeling that had descended over me. I needed time alone to evaluate my thoughts, adjust my thinking, and do something about my double-crossing heart.

"Savannah, aren't you going to sit down with us?"

Uncle Daniel called out to me. "Not on your Nelly," I wanted to shout back. But, of course, that would be rude. So I answered politely.

"No. Sorry. I have something I must do. Please excuse me, everyone," I yelled from the kitchen.

I filled the kettle and put it on to boil. I wasn't sure about anyone else, but I needed a cup of tea and nothing else would do. I stood by the sink and ate my dessert standing up. The kettle finally boiled, and I brewed myself a cup of tea. I set it aside to cool a little and breezed into the dining room again.

"Anyone… for coffee?"

The men looked at me as if I had offered them deadly nightshade. They turned their noses up at my offer. I shrugged my shoulders and was about to go back into the kitchen.

"Something a little stronger… would be nice," Mr Stein beamed, turning a large cigar around between his fingers.

"I second that," said Dr Pitter.

Just in case my darling uncle got the slightest idea of adding his voice. I glared at him with one of my "don't even think of it" look. He seemed to get the picture, for his shoulders shrunk just enough for me to notice.

"I'll be right back," I said, walking out of the dining room and towards my new bedroom.

I could hear footsteps behind me and looked back to see Bobby trailing behind. I hurried as fast as I could, forcing him to run after me. If I was certain of the route to the room, I would have broken into a sprint just to escape. I was surrounded by men, and, right now, only my uncle was safe from a one-way ticket to Siberia.

"Hey, Savannah. What's the rush, man? Wait."

I took the wrong turn and was forced to double back on myself. This, of course, made Bobby's day.

"Don't tell me you're lost again, Savannah!"

He laughed at my confusion, and I made a face and hissed at him.

"This is going to take some getting used to," I said. "This place is as complex as... dear Aunt Eva's ugly mug."

It was meant to be a private thought that had slipped out. Bobby hooted with laughter and volunteered to lead me to my room.

"Follow me, Savannah. I'll lead the way."

Bobby turned in the opposite direction and I followed behind him.

"Savannah, remember, it's a right turn from the dining room to your room, OK?" I curled my upper lip at him. "I think Aunt Eva deliberately made this house to confuse. Let's face it. She wasn't a straightforward woman at all," I reflected, as we walked into the room.

In the boxes I had brought with me, were bottles of spirits and a few bottles of red wine. I was no drinker but did enjoy a glass of good red. The spirits I had brought were for Mr Stein and Ken. I wasn't expecting to see Dr Pitter. I remembered clearly when his wife Amanda died, and I wasn't sure why I had imagined he, too, had died! I would have to share the bottles between them. I went to the largest of the boxes lined up in the sitting room.

"Bobby, come and open this box for me, please," I called.

Bobby, who was nosing around, produced an army knife from his pocket and cut the largest box open. I stood by while he began taking the contents out and putting them on the floor.

"Careful, Bobby. There are bottles in there," I said, as he accidentally dropped a box on the ceramic floor. "That's a stroke of good fortune." I picked up the box and began tearing at the protective bubble wrapping. "It's a bottle of whisky – Scotland's finest." I placed the bottle on a console table by a large window. To distract my thoughts, I peered outside and saw a balcony around the window. "Bobby, is that a balcony I can see out there?" I said, pointing through the window.

"Yeah, it sure is. You have the best in the house. This is a suite."

Wow, I thought. Just the thing to lock myself away whenever I needed to.

"Savannah, you've brought the whole of England with you," Bobby exclaimed from inside the box.

"Not really. I only brought whatever I thought Uncle Daniel would like."

"Yeah. And the rest. Does that include the booze, Savannah?'" Bobby asked, wide-eyed.

"Don't be ridiculous. Of course not. They are presents."

Anyone would have thought I had a brewery in the boxes. Just as well I didn't have them all packed in the same boxes; otherwise Bobby might start thinking I was an alcoholic too.

"Shall I take the bottles through, Savannah?" Bobby asked, holding up a bottle in each hand.

"Those are for Dr Pitter . Get two of the same for Mr Stein, please." I bent down and picked up a box with a bottle of brandy inside. I couldn't present Dr Pitter and Mr Stein with a gift and leave Robin out. I rummaged through another box for a bag of sweets, found one, and held the bag to my nose. I had an incurable sweet tooth and went nowhere without a huge amount of sweets. They said everyone had a vice. I had a couple alright – sweets and falling for the wrong man! "Umm... I can't wait to delve into these," I said, as I waved the bag of sweets in the air.

"What have you got there, Sav?" Bobby grabbed the bag from my hand. "Sweets!" he said with distaste, as if the bag contained some unspeakable sin. I snatched it from his hand and grimaced at him. "Are we done in here now?" he asked. I nodded, and he picked up the bottles. "They'll be in the sitting room... or out on the veranda by now," Bobby added.

"Who... ?" I asked.

"Uncle D… and the others."

"You go and find them. I'll go do the washing up."

"No need, Sav. Ellen would have done that already."

"Umm… will she be staying here? I mean, does she live here?" I asked with condescension in my voice.

I had taken an instant dislike to Ellen. I couldn't think why Uncle Daniel entertained her, for he was a dignified man and was quiet. This woman was larger than life and so were her humongous breasts. I couldn't see how I was going to get along with her at all.

"She might be. It depends on Uncle D."

This made me wonder whether this woman had been living at Peaceful View prior to the fire.

"Erm…" I said, terribly ill at ease.

"Ellen does the domestic's around here, Sav. She always arrives just after dinner."

Well at least, I wouldn't have to sit across the dinner table looking at her mountain of a chest or listening to her suicidal voice.

"I see…"

I guess I would rather dive head first into a bubbling, deep fat fryer than share my space with the frightful Ellen. I had three choices as I saw it: accept the situation, which I wasn't going to, volunteer to do the cleaning myself, or book into a hotel. I mulled the situation over in my head as I followed Bobby back to the sitting room.

As we walked through the door, we found the four men standing over a drinks trolley in the corner – each with glass in hand. Uncle Daniel was the last to turn around and face us. My eyes locked into his as if in combat, and his earlier mellowed expression vanished. Like someone caught on the wrong side of the law, his face took on a mask of unadulterated guilt.

CHAPTER 15

"There you are. We wondered where you'd got to," Mr Stein exclaimed, as Bobby and I appeared at the sitting room door.

I looked at the trolley laden down with all manner of local brew and passed a disapproving eye over my uncle. Then I stood back and allowed Bobby to share the bottles of spirit between Dr Pitter and Mr Stein.

"Savannah, how very thoughtful, my dear. Did you guess my supplies were running low?"

Dr Pitter showed his appreciation, and I was only too glad he was still with us. I wouldn't reveal the fact I had thought he was dead. I don't think Dr Pitter would be impressed if he was to find out I had killed him off!

"Oh… it's my pleasure, Dr Pitter. I'm so glad to have you with us."

We hugged each other warmly.

"It's my turn now, young lady."

Mr Stein affectionately nudged Dr Pitter out of the way in order to reach me.

"Again... it's my pleasure, Mr Stein. I hope you will enjoy them."

He took both my hands and kissed them respectively. I smiled at the good manners of both men who were from what Grandma would have called, "the old school." I guess I was still stuck in an era that had died; only I refused to bury it. Bobby and Robin were deep in hushed conversation at the other end of the room. I approached and gave Robin the box in my hand. He knew instantly what was inside and grinned in that boyish manner that made him so incredibly attractive. Then he winked at me again, and my blooming legs began to shake. "OK, Savannah. Keep your head. He is only a man. Not God," a voice whispered into my ear.

"Savannah... how very kind," he said, taking both my hands the way Mr Stein had done earlier.

I just knew he was going to go one further. I looked up at him with what I hoped was an expressionless face. I felt the warmth of his cheek brush against the back of one hand before his lips connected on the first, and then the second hand. I smiled civilly, and then extracted my hands from his grasp. I rushed across the room to stand by Uncle Daniel's chair, putting a safe enough distance between Robin and me. I began to observe Dr Pitter and Mr Stein in turn.

Both had been faithful friends of my grandparents. When Grandma died, it was to Mr Stein I had turned. He gladly took over and oversaw the yearly payment of taxes for Peaceful View, kept me up-to date on the happenings on the island, and generally kept an eye on Uncle Daniel for me. I not only loved him dearly, I saw him as family. Then there was Dear Dr Pitter – the family's doctor and a close friend. He was one of the only two people who really knew me as a child and whose trust and tender care saw me through the worst years of my life. He taught me to express my thoughts and feelings in drawings and stories, and he gave me my very first diary. My love of poetry began with a book of poems he had presented to me as a reward for finding his loved silver pen. As a child, I had formed a deep bond with both him and his late wife Amanda. I felt privileged to have them there and looked forward to many happy hours of small talk with them both. I had to turn my head away, for I was inundated with the bitter-sweet memories of a time that was never going to come back.

"Well, gentlemen... what will it be?" Bobby asked, gesturing towards the trolley.

Mr Stein was first to respond. He held out his empty glass and pointed excitedly to the whisky bottle.

"I'd love a tot of the old scotch fire please, young Bobby."

I remembered the once younger Gus Stein. He must be in his late seventies now. But apart from his cotton wool white hair, his skin was as supple and line free as it was when I last saw him over twenty years earlier. I felt both touched and honoured to see that life had been kind to him. His white hair and jowl cheeks were the only telltale signs of ageing.

"Savannah, my dear... are you going to have a little tipple?"

I smiled at Dr Pitter and shook my head before answering, "I only drink a glass or two of red wine. Other than that, I don't drink."

"That is very sensible, my dear."

He raised his whisky glass at me, and I gave him the thumbs up. Like Uncle Daniel, Dr Pitter had aged but had not lost his spirit or his caring bedside manner. His gentle nature remained and he spoke in the same soft tone I remembered so very well. I could feel my emotions heightening and wanted to leave the men to enjoy each other's company as if I wasn't there. I tapped Uncle Daniel on the shoulder. He was the only one without a glass now. The one I had caught him with had mysteriously vanished from his hand. I gestured for him to follow me out of the room. He stood up.

"I am excusing myself, gentlemen. My niece wants a word in my ear."

We swapped the sitting room for the dining room, and I closed the door behind us. It was no point beating about the bush. I got straight to the point.

"Uncle Daniel, I won't preach to you. I just want to ask that you cut down on your drinking."

I watched his expression keenly and believed I saw relief on his face – relief for having being caught or relief I might be aware of his drinking problem.

"Savannah... princess... I will do anything for you, anything."

"Uncle Daniel, you have to do this for yourself." I led him to a chair and he sat down.

"Try loving yourself, Uncle Daniel. Stop punishing yourself for things you cannot change," I pleaded. I knew my uncle's life centred on the guilt he carried concerning his mother's illness and eventual death. Neither one of us could change what had happened nor could one of us bring Grandma back. Allowing guilt to eat away at our souls was to show a lack of appreciation for the precious gift of life. To drink himself into an early grave would solve nothing. If I were beginning to come to terms with the loss of Grandma, Uncle Daniel would have to try and do the same.

The only person who could restore Grandma back to life was God, and God would do that in his own time. I sat down in front of Uncle Daniel and rested my hands on my lap.

"After dinner in the evenings, you can have two single shots. Don't have alcohol for breakfast, lunch, or dinner anymore – understood?" My uncle nodded his head like a naughty little boy caught with his dirty hand down the cookie jar.

"You can choose whether you have them together or spread them out. Say, perhaps, one before dinner and one after… it's your choice. You can swap the shorts for a beer, if you prefer. Again… the choice is yours."

The vulnerability I saw on his face was breaking my heart, for I knew only too well what pains he carried in his heart. I did not want to treat him like a child but had no choice. I wanted him alive – not dead. I wanted the chance to spend a few years with him, to help him heal, and perhaps find happiness even. If I can help him to forget that terrible night that haunted us both, then I would have achieved peace for both of us. It was time we both shed the burden of guilt.

"Do we understand each other, Uncle Daniel?" He nodded and I suspected he, too, had sat visualising the night Grandma took the blow that was to bring about her demise. Over the years, Uncle Daniel and I had been fighting a loosing battle as each tried in vain to wrestle the guilt away from the other. In truth, the guilt was all mine. If I had stayed out of Claude's way, there would not have been a fight between the brothers. I had strayed into Claude's path, as I often did, without intending to, and, as always, Claude had struck out at me. This time, the utter mindlessness of Claude's brutality against me; drove Uncle

Daniel over the edge. A vicious fight broke out between the brothers, and Grandma had to jump between her sons. The blow meant for Claude had smashed into Grandma's face. Days later, she suffered a stroke, and, from this point on, my once robust grandmother's health deteriorated. Her death three years later left us both unable to come to terms with our guilt.

"I will trust you to keep your promise. But the minute I find you've gone back on your word, I'll be on my way to the airport... never to return here again."

Uncle Daniel gagged on my words. He frowned as if in pain and his eyes jutted out. I felt like the cruel angel of doom who had just delivered a message of destruction to a way of life he had become accustomed to. But if I got the desired effect I sought, then my message of doom would be worth every painful moment. It was time we set ourselves free.

"OK, princess. You have my word. I'll do anything for you... anything."

I heard anxiety in Uncle Daniel's voice and knew I had hit home. If he was prepared to quit his destructive habit for me, I was prepared to go along with it until he was strong enough to do it for himself. Getting him to this point was an achievement within itself. He had turned to the bottle on the Sunday afternoon I had found Grandma slumped on the floor in the summer house. I was eight years old and was soon to leave the island for England.

"OK. You better get back to the boys before they send out a search party."

He got to his feet, and then pulled me into an embrace.

"I love you very much, Savannah. What other incentive do I need to clean up myself and my miserable life? I want to see you married... with children."

He held me away from him, and I could see the doting great uncle with the patience of Job. I hoped one day soon I would be able to give him this wish. My children would be to him the grandchildren he'd never had, and I would love that more than anything. I believed my uncle was on his way to an alcohol-free diet. I planned to support him every step of the way. I stood up and waved him out of the dining room with hope in my heart. All I needed to do now - was to find that husband.

"Off you go. I'm going to make some tea, and then come and say goodnight."

He nodded at me and disappeared on his way back into the sitting room. I wasn't going to make it obvious I would be watching him – but I would be. With the men retired to the comfort of Aunt Eva's huge and sumptuous sitting room, I went into the kitchen to make myself another cup of tea. The kitchen was spotless with no signs of the mountain of dirty dishes I had left piled up in the sink. I saw no signs of Ellen, though, and wondered whether Uncle Daniel had told her to make herself scarce. I put the kettle on, and while I waited for it to boil, I spent my time gazing out the kitchen window.

My mind turned back to Mr Stein and Dr Pitter. Both would be expecting me to attend the local Anglican church. My family had been members of the congregation – going back to two sets of great grandparents who were buried in the grounds of the old church. Grandma had been faithful to both church and faith until the last stroke had put her to bed. I would have to go in respect of their memory. It would be considered disrespectful otherwise. The thought triggered a dilemma as I rummaged through the contents of my suitcases, in my mind. With no prior thought of church, I had packed not a single suitable item of clothing!

Light easy-to-wash summer clothes and party frocks that would be looked upon as immodest were what I had packed! As my imagination overdosed on the contents of my suitcases, I wondered how I would manage. It was possible I might be able to solve the problem of a hat. I had seen at least half a dozen hat boxes on top of the wardrobes in Aunt Eva's bedroom. But then again, if the hats belonged to my Aunt Eva, I'd need a round washing-up bowl for a head. I'd just have to change the whole concept of the sombre dress code expected for church!

I'd have the whole congregation vying for my blood once again. For I would have to strut my stuff into church, dressed in a pair of shorts, a boob tube, or a backless number and a baseball cap. The younger members of the congregation would secretly applaud my daring, while the older, more restrained no-nonsense ones would demand my expulsion yet again! I could almost hear the whispers and feel hot sticky eyes burning into my back.

Others would peer at me with disdain and snigger to each other,

"What dishonour! This is blasphemy! Jane Holness-Duncan's bones must turn in her grave! But then, did we really expect anything better from that devilish child?! Sister… do you remember how many times that obstinate girl was thrown out of this church? Her behaviour gave her poor grandmother some terrible turns. Worst still, was she not the same one who'd set fire to the vestry! Dug up her dead aunt and brought her army of animals into church?!

Did she not trip up Pastor Mac and stand on the visiting vicar's robe choking the poor reverend half to death! Do you remember the time she filled the baptismal pool with earth so she could bury a dead mongoose? Was she not expelled until she could behave herself? Oh… and do you remember, sister, when she told brother Samuda to…? Well, she was no more than five or six at the time. That girl was never normal. That's why Pastor Mac had condemned her to hell. "

Yes. They would all recall the atrocious things I had done as a child – except for a handful perhaps. I giggled to myself as my mind switched from the congregation to the cynical Dick, Aunt Rebecca's husband. He would have been proud of my thoughts. Grandma once caught him as he taught me his version of Christianity.

"Vannah," he had said, "there is no one up there. It's a story told by old men with long white beards – drunk out of their heads on white rum. What I dislike most around here is all the rules. I like the way you break every one of them, though. You don't give a fiddlers fart for any rules, do you, Vannah? My reckoning is, you can't have rules unless someone breaks them now and then. Upset the balance a bit."

My giggles soon turned to downright laughter as I visualised myself in church. Completely lost in my own weird and sometimes wonderful world of thoughts, I was oblivious to all around me. I could hear Dick's voice in my head as if we sat together. Then, out of the blue, reality hit me like a brick in the head.

My solitary moment was quickly brought to an abrupt end when an unambiguous voice behind me asked, "Am I to stand here watching you laugh yourself into a stupor, Savannah? Won't you share the joke with me?"

CHAPTER 16

I turned around to see Robin standing in the kitchen doorway. In each of his hands was a glass. He winked at me, and then, as he held out the glass with the rum punch to me, a mischievous grin played across his face

"A nightcap, Ms Hanson – to relax you."

"I beg your pardon?" I replied, more than a little curious as to what the meaning behind his remark might be.

"Savannah, I sense you were tense earlier… uptight," Robin said with a more sombre expression on his face. My moody answer had wiped the grin clean from off his face.

"I am uptight because I feel uncomfortable with the situation I find myself in – who wouldn't?" I said, sourly.

I detected the ringing of a discrete alarm bell in my head. However, as a matter of courtesy, I took the glass from his hand.

"Thank you… but don't make a habit of this."

I took a tiny sip, smacked my lips, and rolled my eyes in mock drunkenness. Two glasses, and I had difficulty seeing, let alone standing. My head would take off in one direction while the rest of my body struggled to remain on terra firma. Most of the time however, I embarrass myself by throwing up.

Robin's boyish grin returned instantly. He raised his glass in my direction. I returned the gesture, raising my own glass; then I put it down on the work surface next to me. As appetising as the rum punch was, and as much as I do enjoy a small glass, I had no intention of allowing my wayward thoughts to be manipulated by alcohol. I have never forgotten its lucid effect on my tongue or the heady and stupefying feelings, which accompanied the very smell.

"I have a question I'd like to ask… if I'm permitted… that is?" said Robin.

"What do you want to know, Robin?"

I was curious, for his mood was in all probability, influenced by the brandy in his hand.

"Why are you hiding out here? It's noticeable, you know."

A transient smile passed over my face with the question. I wouldn't quite call it hiding; it was more a case of putting space between Robin and me. I decided to answer his question with one of my own.

"What makes you think I am hiding? And what is there to hide from?"

"I clearly remember asking you a question, Savannah. It seems you're afraid of your own answer."

He was more serious now as he raised the brandy glass to his lips. I observed his facial changes but made no reply. I had sensed Robin was easily bruised and was probably a very sensitive man.

"OK, Savannah. We'll come back to my question. At least tell me… why you were laughing to yourself when I first got here?"

I sighed one of those half laugh half sighs, which caused a sound to rise up from the throat. If I was to give Robin an insight into my off-the-rails thoughts, he might think me more than a little unhinged. I wasn't ready to be sent off to the happy farm just yet. I turned away from him momentarily; for I was almost tempted to tell him why I had been laughing. I decided to leave it, though, until he got a bit more used to my sometimes crazy sense of humour.

"Won't you share the joke with me, Savannah?" he asked again as if desperate to know what floated my boat.

"Umm…It's nothing… really. Just my thoughts playing games with me," I answered. A slight droop touched one corner of his lovely mouth, and then a pensive shadow clouded his gorgeous face. I was sure Robin was sulking, like a little boy who'd just handed over his prized marble having lost a wager to his friend. If I knew him well enough, I would believe I had hurt his feelings. I picked up the glass of rum punch although I had no intention of drinking it. For a time, I looked down into the strawberry-coloured liquid in quiet acknowledgement, for this was no average beverage. It was one to be treated with the utmost respect. I yanked my thoughts away from the glass in my hand and set my eyes on his face again. In spite of Robin's sensitiveness, I could have walked straight into the alluring depths of his strangely beautiful eyes, set up a comfortable home, and refused to be rescued even if his eyes had caught fire.

Instead of following my ruinous heart, which urged me to take that walk towards him, I began to pray silently. I shook the thought right out of my head. I had more important things to occupy my mind. An oversensitive man who sulked if he couldn't have what he wanted wasn't my idea of fun. I toyed with the glass between my fingers. It was something to do with my idle hands, for I had called to mind my childhood exploits with the wicked white rum. Looking back, it was almost inconceivable I used to binge on it in my moments of despair. I often sat stupefied high up in the eastern hills. There, I was safe from Claude. The only soul who knew my whereabouts was my faithful dog Whisky.

The last time Uncle Daniel had found me smashed, I was still clutching a half flask bottle of rum, a half-smoked Havana cigar, and a box of matches. On that occasion, I had been missing for three days. The combination of rum and cigar had knocked me out cold. It was to be the last time I touched anything alcoholic. When I was seventeen, my father placed a bottle of Baby Cham in my hand.

"Happy birthday, Savannah," he had said.

Oddly, this is the only time I could recall my father showing an interest in me or acknowledging my birthday. I had second thoughts about another taste. I swilled the drink around in the glass, and then emptied it down the drain. It was potent stuff, and I needed to keep my mind and thoughts under tight control. How anyone could develop a liking for this or any alcoholic concoction, I simply couldn't imagine.

"No reflection on you. Robin. Let's just say – I had a disquieting visit from an old memory."

"You had a drink problem… in the past, Savannah?"

He appeared to be preparing himself, for his mood changed in an instant. This man changed moods more often than a chameleon's camouflages. He grew pensive or perhaps, even shocked. I figured he had adjusted his mindset in preparing for what he thought might be some murky confession from my past. I wasn't going to let him down, for what I was about to tell him, wouldn't disappoint.

"Yeah… I guess you could say that."

As my answer registered in his mind, his expression changed yet again. He seemed knocked for six at my admission. After all, I had to admit, I must have been the most unlikely-looking ex-alcoholic on the planet. I expected him to begin questioning me, but his questions dried up with my answer. He just looked at me.

"I had no idea at the time I had a problem. It was years later that I realised. It must have started when I was five… I'm not sure. It ended when I was roughly eight or so."

I turned away from his glare to stare out the kitchen window, and then up at the night sky. I hoped to see an expanse of stars twinkling their awesome light at me. Darkness had already set in with its thick gloom. I gazed up at the heavens now, but it disappointed me. The heavens were still a mass of disturbing grey rain clouds. My eyes fell on the hills below; I wondered what unspeakable secrets were hidden in the hills around Peaceful View half hidden under the shadows of a night such as this; the hills I found so intensely alluring during daylight appeared disquietingly supernatural under the cover of darkness.

In the thick gloominess outside, night creatures were in full swing. They competed with each other to make the weirdest racket in the hills. They droned on in their unsystematic chorus in the dark recesses of their bush homes. I turned away from the window and shifted a little distance away, for I had the oddest sensation of being watched. My thoughts turned inward as memories of Claude lined up in front of my eyes, and my mood changed to mirror the blackness of the night. Memories of Claude were the ones I tried desperately not to recall.

They were what my nightmares were made of. I glanced at Robin who, it seemed, was watching me closely.

"I had no idea what I was doing at the time. I used to hit the bottle whenever…"

I must have appeared forlorn for Robin took a few steps closer to where I stood by the sink. I held up one hand to ward him off.

"Keep talking, Savannah," he said swallowing down the brandy. He placed the empty glass in the kitchen sink next to me. I began washing both glasses as a distraction – buying myself time. I was about to give Robin a tiny peek into the areas of darkness I kept sealed off from all – even my closest friend and confidant Marin.

"Whenever Claude came back to Peaceful View. I knew I was in for it. I would slip a flask or two from the shop when Dick wasn't looking. I hid my stash in the hills. Each time Claude harmed me… whether it was a kick, a pinch, a cigarette burn, or…"

I had to take a breath, for I had tried to break free from the chains of these particular memories once before and had failed miserably. I wasn't prepared to travel down that road again.

"Go on, Savannah. Get it out… let it go," counselled Robin.

Oddly, I found for the first time that I really did want to open my heart and set myself free. I began to pace the floor.

"I'd disappear into the hills and drink the rum I had hidden there. It didn't make me feel very good, but it made me loose consciousness. I'd sleep for hours – days sometimes."

I looked up suddenly, for I felt a hand on my shoulder; but it was too late. I was already in Robin's arms. His chin nestled on top of my head, as though it belonged there. I felt at home against his masculine chest. His embrace was firm yet tender and comforting. I felt protected by him. I was enclosed in his arms, and the feeling was the most natural feeling to me. I could have stayed against him till the end of time. But I was supposed to be practical and was a hopeless realist. In addition, he was someone else's husband. I pushed him away.

"Don't do that again… ever," I whispered.

The poor confused man held his hands up the way I had done earlier; I saw exasperation on his face.

"Sorry I offended you. However, my intensions were honourable, Savannah," he said brusquely.

I was sure if he could have whipped himself for touching me, he would have.

"Yes, I know they are. I'm the problem… Sorry."

I was the one riddled with fear, mistrust, and guilt. I was projecting my feelings on to him because I didn't trust anything resembling a man – with the exception of Martin and my uncle. Maybe this was the reason the right man never came along for I would not be able to spot him through my tangled and ever-changing web of feelings.

"I had no idea you had such a tough time, Savannah. Was my father aware?"

"No need to feel sorry. I'm not looking for sympathy. And, yes, Dr Pitter knew all about it. Your mother did too."

"Good Heavens! What a dreadful tale."

"It's no tale. It's real… and save your pity, for I don't need it. Anymore of it, and I will shut you out."

"No, please. I want to hear it all."

And what good would my childhood melancholies do for you? I asked in my head.

"Then no pitying words. Save your pity for…" I wanted to say "for your unhappy marriage," but I was certain my uncle would have hung and quartered me from either the lychee or the tamarind trees. I held back, biting my tongue, for I had no right, whatsoever, to be angry at this man. He wasn't the source of the pains I carried deep inside my heart. I felt guilty for being horrid to him.

"Robin, I am truly sorry. Please accept my apology."

I wanted to run from the kitchen and hide away in shame.

"I am not certain why you believe I pity you. Nothing could be further from the truth. You need no pity at all. The moment I set eyes on you, I sensed you were deep… or perhaps a little vulnerable. Pity never entered my mind. You need… no pity. What you need is release. You're forgiven on the condition you start trusting me."

I sighed. Robin might be the exception, for while I may open up and tell him about my childhood pains, I wasn't going to trust him with my heart. He had the look of a sexual predator about him; he claimed to be unhappy in his marital life, yet refused to face up to reality.

"Savannah, I'm sorry if I have awakened memories you'd rather left forgotten," Robin said, as I walked back to the window.

The squalls that had been going on for sometime seemed to be gathering pace now. I adored the rains and the peaceful aura it sent to wrap itself about me. If it continued throughout the night, I was guaranteed a blissful night's sleep. I turned back to face him. I wondered how he would act if I was to unleash the details of my heart in one fell swoop.

"Not to worry, Robin. My childhood's not any fault of yours."

He looked at me with hopeful eyes, and I was glad to see the darkness lifting from his face.

"I know I need to get these awful memories out of my system. I want to move on."

"Shall we go somewhere else so we can talk?"

It was a genuine no-strings-attached question. I nodded. He turned towards the kitchen door and I followed. I soon realised he was heading in the direction of the set of rooms Uncle Daniel had moved me into. We crossed the corridor towards the large door that opened on to another corridor, and then the sitting room. There was a door on either side of the sitting room, which I guessed, were the rooms Uncle Daniel and Robin would be sleeping in. I remembered the sitting room we were about to enter was no longer neatly arranged, for the contents from two of the boxes Bobby and me had opened earlier were strewn over the floor.

"I better warn you, it's a mess in there," I said, yawning.

I suddenly felt really sleepy.

"You don't strike me as a messy pup, Savannah," he said, as we reached the door. He turned the lock and stepped aside for me to enter first.

"See, I did warn you," I said, gesturing with my hand in the direction of the boxes and their contents.

I was no Snow White, if that's what he thought. In addition to my four boxes and three suitcases, there was a stack of what I called "solicitors boxes"; they were numbered 1-13 and were neatly arranged under one window.

"What are those? They aren't mine. How did they get here?"

"Those are your grandmother's papers, Savannah. They are yours now."

"Oh… hogwash. I can't deal with them tonight. In fact, I don't want to deal with them at all."

I rushed towards the door, but Robin's hand caught up with me before I even got close enough to touch the lock...

"Savannah, we were going to talk. Have you forgotten?"

The sight of those boxes containing my grandmother's private papers were enough to unnerve me. I was completely thrown off guard. I was never going to be able to deal with them; it was too final and I wasn't ready to say good-bye.

"Robin, the boxes... do I need to go through them? Is it necessary?"

"Not if you're not ready. I can talk you through the contents— not all of them, mind."

"All right. But not tonight. I can't face it yet."

He nodded, and I saw sympathy in his eyes. At least he understood, I thought to myself. I know I will have to face those boxes one day but had no idea when that would be. I walked to the window at the other end of the same wall. I lifted the curtains and looked out into the night. It dawned on me that the hurricane season was in full swing, and a tiny shiver ran through me. I watched the rapidly-darkened heavens and wondered whether a hurricane was heading our way. Along with lightning, a hurricane was another of my fears. I have never experienced one but was certain it must be among the most terrifying occurrences in nature. After all, nature was terribly fickle and could be mindlessly cruel.

"Can I come in?"

Robin answered the knock that followed the voice at the door. I turned around to see Uncle Daniel in the room.

"Just checking to see if I am needed," Uncle Daniel said.

I knew he was talking to Robin, so I made no reply.

"No. I think we better leave it for a while yet, Daniel."

I went to a chair and sat down.

"Another day or two, perhaps," said Robin.

As if weighing up my present state of mind, he looked deep into my eyes. A part of me wanted to get tonight over with, but something inside my heart just wasn't willing. Uncle Daniel came and sat on the arm of my chair.

"Savannah, we must do this soon. Robin and I have some important things to talk to you about."

"I know. I will talk with you. But not now – not tonight."

"Alright. But soon. Promise."

I nodded and looked across at Robin. I saw concern under eyebrows that arched in a puzzled frown. I knew straight away that I was going to break my promise to Bobby.

"Alright, princess. I'll leave you in Robin's capable hands. I better go and get some extra rooms ready. No one will be leaving here tonight on account of the weather."

"Alright, Daniel. I will see you in a while."

I waved at my uncle as he and Robin walked to the door. The two men talked in quiet tones. Then Robin closed the door and came to sit in the chair opposite me. It was now or never.

"Robin, I know of the threat to my life. Bobby told me. I don't want him to get into trouble, though. Please don't tell Uncle Daniel."

I watched Robin's reactions. He seemed to be mulling what I said over in his mind before making a reply.

"Savannah, we don't want you worrying unnecessarily. We don't know for certain. What we do know, however, is that Claude cannot be trusted."

"I know that more than anybody else, Robin. You don't have to remind me."

I wasn't being rude; I was just stating a fact. I carried the scars, not to mention the memories that had stunted my perception and trust in people – men in particular. Whilst the memories that haunted me weren't all of Claude's making – for there were connotations of my father too – the nightmares were mostly about Claude.

"Savannah, I don't want you to be afraid. However, you must be careful while you are here."

"Are you saying I am going to be a prisoner here?"

"No. I am not saying that at all. I am saying you must be careful. No wandering off into the hills or bushes for that matter. I have some time to spare and will be dividing my time between here and home. I was wondering whether you might like to spend some time with me and Daddy in Montego Bay. We have a house there."

Robin showed no surprise at my knowledge. It was as though he expected me to have known about the threat to my life. He did not appear overly alarmed. I couldn't read what his thoughts might be. He showed no facial expressions to betray his thoughts. However, I saw no signs of anxiety in Robin's expressions nor had I detected any in his voice. Bobby might just be viewing me as a threat. He had his twenty acres of land now. What else could he possibly want? Another twenty acres, perhaps? He could have that too. I breathed a sigh of relief. For whilst I was terrified of Claude, Bobby was small change I could jingle in my pockets, if I so wished.

"Let me think about your offer, Robin. It might be too soon to run off and leave Uncle Daniel. I want to spend some time alone with him. Just the two of us. It's a nice thought. I'll definitely come back to you on it."

"I understand, Savannah. Daniel will love every moment of your company. He thinks the world of you."

"Yes, I know. I'm the closest he will get to having a child of his own. Bless his heart."

Robin smiled knowingly, and I wondered if my uncle had spoken to him about me over the years.

"Robin, has your father said anything about the state of Uncle Daniel's health?"

"Savannah, I am sure Daddy will speak to you if there's a problem."

Umm… short and sweet, I thought.

"I got the picture. I won't press you further."

It was time for me to lock myself away in my room. I was tired and needed a little time alone.

"Robin, would you mind if we continue our conversation in the morning? I'm getting sleepy."

I noted my request seemed to have taken him by surprise; he looked wounded. I was genuinely tired, though, and hoped he would see that and understand.

"I'm disappointed you are going to bed so soon. Jetlag has set in, perhaps. I know that feeling well myself."

He immediately stood up, ready to go. I liked that. I didn't need to come up with an excuse for Robin to go.

"I have to say good night to everyone. I will follow you back to the sitting room."

We walked back to the sitting room together in a comfortable silence. There we found the men all slumped in various armchairs; they were clutching their glasses to their chests. I was relieved to see Uncle Daniel was the only one without a glass. I am sure it must be hard for him to resist, but I was proud to see he was at least trying. Still, I gave him one of my questioning looks, and he shook his head discretely. I walked over to him and placed a hand on his shoulder to show my support.

"I want to say good night before I fall asleep on my feet," I whispered into his ear, and then gave him a peck on the cheek.

I turned towards Dr Pitter and Mr Stein, who sat side by side; they were almost consumed by the huge armchairs they sat in.

"Good night to you both," I said, kissing them each.

Finally, it was Bobby's turn.

"I'm the eternal party pooper, Bobby. I am whacked. I'm going straight to bed." I said, yawning.

"Night, Sav. See you in the morning."

I waved good night from the doorway, and Robin followed me back to my room. "Thank you for listening to me, Robin. And sorry if I was rude. It wasn't intended."

"You get off to bed. I will be turning in shortly myself. I have some papers with me that I must read tonight. If you find yourself awake in the middle of the night, I'm next door."

He pointed to the door to our left.

"Ah… yes. Uncle Daniel did say he would be on one side of me, with you on the other. Well, at least I can sleep soundly with you both watching over me."

He smiled, and his autumn eyes appeared to light up the space around us.

"We will pick up where we left off tomorrow… I promise. Good night, Robin, sleep well."

I closed the door and went through the sitting room and into my bedroom. The rooms on either side, where Uncle Daniel and Robin would be sleeping, had connecting doors directly into the sitting room. I would have to be mindful not to wander there half naked in the dead of night, I thought to myself.

CHAPTER 17

I opened the door to my bedroom and knew instantly that someone had been there ahead of me. In addition, the bed had been turned down; I wasn't happy at all. As irrelevant as it might appear, it was one intrusion too many. I saw it as an invasion – as if I had been violated. I would have to speak to Uncle Daniel about it first thing in the morning. I consoled myself, for I did not want to go to bed feeling upset. I prayed for my annoyance to leave me, and then went into the bathroom to have a shower.

Feeling refreshed after my shower, I climbed into a pair of light cotton pyjamas. I was about to get into bed when that voice in my head told me to check the room. I pulled everything off the bed, shook each piece one by one, and then replaced them. I did the same with the two pillows. Removing the pillowcases, I shook them vigorously before putting them back on again. Then of all things to do, I checked underneath the bed and behind the curtains – giving them a shake. I opened the closet doors and searched that thoroughly too. Finally, I did the same with the rugs on both sides of my bed. Once I felt content all was well, I went back into the bathroom and washed my hands. Satisfied there was no one in the room or any foreign bodies waiting to pounce, I climbed into bed.

At the beginning of the year, I had embarked on the task of reading the Bible from beginning to end. My intention was to complete the entire Bible by the year's end. Being brought up on the holy writing from as far back as I can remember; I already had both love and deep respect for my Creator. My understandings of the Bible, however, were conflicting due to my early experience in the Anglican church. There the true meaning of God's words was replaced with the despicable interpretations of men. My memories of Pastor Mac had left me disillusioned and afraid. For years I would only pick up my Bible on odd occasions. Though nothing could shake my belief in God, I had lost commitment to the faith I had been born into. I had not seen the inside of a church for a long while and had no desire to do so. Since I was banned from our local Anglican church as a child, I had only gone to church twice. On these occasions, it was to attend a wedding. The last wedding was that of my cousin Rachael. I had vowed then that it would be the last time I entered a building of oppression.

As I began reading the scriptures, I became more and more fascinated with each discovery. I was convinced, there was much more to life than the conventional churches would have me believe. I could not comprehend the reasoning behind evolution when creation dispelled the theory so literally. Man being born a helpless baby and then growing in strength and vigour only to shrivel up and die didn't add up. I wanted to know why we grew old and died. The cruel ravages of the aging process made no sense to me at all. The evidence creation presented suggested that someone with a colossal capacity to love made us with a purpose.

I wanted to know why we were put here on this copious earth. But, above all, I felt a seething gripe about the excessive cruelty of ageing. I resented this process with such venom that it became an obsession until I took control and tried to find answers. I soon realised that the source of the answers could not be found in jars, bottles, or a surgeon's scalpel. The person who created man in the first place was the source I sought. The answer was right under my nose. If I truly wanted to gain understanding, I had to get an insight into the mind of God. And this would be through the Bible. I had to understand why God, who so lovingly made us in his own image and put us on a bounteous earth with everything to sustain us, could turn around and allow us to suffer the indignity of old age and death.

Anticipation welled up inside now as I arranged the pillows to sit right. I wanted to be as comfortable as I could get. I leaned across the bedside table and collected up my Bible. Then I lay back to read The Prophet Isaiah's writings. So far, I had been reading my way through with gripping interest. As each chapter unfolded, my understanding and knowledge grew. This in turn fanned the flames of love in my heart. The force that had compelled me to explore the meaning of life now urged me to read on.

****

Now and then I closed my Bible to meditate on what I had read. I thought of the lie I had believed for years: that I was destined to go to hell because I was deemed bad and that only good people went to heaven. I discovered that only a certain number, namely 144,000, would actually go to heaven. My mind turned to the miracle of pregnancy and birth. I patted my tummy in anticipation of the day a precious life would grow there. I thought of the various emotions and tender compassion we all possessed; man's insatiable appetite to have a mate to love and to be loved in return; the body's ability to heal itself; the amazing feeling I would get whenever I gazed up at a star-studded night sky; the simple pleasures of a sunset or sunrise; the wonders of a full moon on a cloudless night; and the beauty of flowers with their intricate designs.

I smiled to myself as I ruminated. I thought of the air we breathe and the bountiful collection of humans, animals, and plants. I marvelled to myself as I turned my attention on the elements outside.

My eyes fell on the curtains. Every now and then they were billowed outwards as the restless wind crashed against the windows. From time to time, the wind whistled and sent movable objects scurrying into the night, while the rains played sweet soothing music on the roof. I had cracked open the window nearest my bed and wondered whether I should close it. But, instead, I slid further down under the covers. Sleepy eyed and struggling to stay awake, I moved my precious book of knowledge to safety. Just before sleep took me away on a journey of renewal, I pondered on the verses I had selected as my sleep partner: Isaiah 65:17-25. I liked these verses for here was additional proof that God loved the human race and had created us with a purpose. I turned out the nightlight and journeyed into the wonderful world of sleep.

"Savannah... are you awake?"

An unanticipated intervention pulled me out from under the covers.

"The door is open. Come in."

His head appeared around the door, and then the rest of him followed. He came over to sit on my bed. I smiled a sleepy smile and rubbed my eyes to bring them back to life.

"Are you alright, princess? Are you comfortable?"

"Yes. Divinely comfortable. Thank you."

He put down a bunch of keys on the bedside table next to my Bible.

"I see you haven't forsaken the good book, princess."

Uncle Daniel picked up my Bible and flicked through the pages I had marked.

"How could I? It would be sacrilege. Grandma's bones would rattle in the earth if I dared. Besides, I have been drawn to my spiritual side of late."

I yawned sleepily.

"You were always curious about life, Savannah. You must have been the only child I knew who would sit and read the books of Revelation. The rest of us avoided it."

I smiled at the memory of the goosebumps that used to crawl all over me as fear of the Revelations took hold. I understood very little at the time and could hardly pronounce some words. I had to run back and forth to Grandma so she could tell me how to say the words I couldn't get my tongue around.

"Do you know, Uncle Daniel, I was terrified of what I read at the time. I know better now, though. The Revelations are wonderful news if you take the time to read and understand it."

"I avoid it. It's far too powerful. I find it..."

Uncle Daniel probably meant to say "frightening", but it wouldn't have been the manly thing to admit.

"Then I will help you to understand it. You will be amazed at its meaning."

"Alright. I look forward to that."

I reached forward and stroked his face.

"Everyone's gone to bed. Nothing has changed. The whole island goes to bed early and then wakes up early."

I remembered prayers in Grandma's bedroom when I was a child. By eight at night, we would assemble around Grandma's huge brass bed for family prayers. Once prayers were over, we would say good night to each other and head to our individual bedrooms. The younger children would be sent to bed at eight-thirty while the adults drifted away between nine and nine-thirty.

"You are comfortable, aren't you, princess?"

I nodded again for I couldn't be more comfortable if I tried.

"The doors are locked for the night. You must lock this door once I leave. I will wait outside to make sure you obey," he said jokingly but I had a feeling it wasn't a joke. Uncle Daniel got up to go, and I was forced out from my comfort zone. I followed him to the door.

"Night… princess."

He cupped my face in the palms of his hands and kissed me on the forehead.

"Night night, Papa," I said quite unexpectedly.

My beloved uncle's weathered face transformed. If Uncle Daniel had suffered sleeplessness in the past, tonight he was going to sleep like a baby. He was thrilled to be called "Papa" again. I closed the door and turned the key noisily in the lock to convince him I had locked the door. I smiled my way back to bed feeling truly humbled by my dear uncle's pleasure. I slipped under the covers once more and fell asleep.

******

I woke in the early hours with a desperate urge to go back to the remains of the house. I had not been near it since the afternoon I had arrived to find it smouldering in grey-black ashes. Then, I had refused to look too closely at the remains. If I had, I would have had to accept my loss. This morning, however, I woke knowing I had to go back. I sat up and listened for signs of life. But all was quiet. I got out of bed as quietly as I could and pulled the bedcovers back. I crept into the bathroom, where I brushed my teeth and washed my face. I slapped on some moisturiser and went back into the bedroom. I made my bed and then picked up my Bible again. Holding it in both hands, I prayed for

God's guidance. Then I allowed the pages to fall open randomly. The pages fell open at Psalms 15. I began to read.

******

 I dressed appropriately in jeans and a cotton shirt and then crept to the back door. After opening the door, I was faced with a heavily-grilled gate. I tackled it with trepidation, for I thought I might wake everyone up. The very first key I tried, however, sent the lock flying back. I said a silent thank you in my heart and stepped outside. I locked both the door and the grill behind me. My watch registered a quarter to five. I set off. I needed this calm time alone for my almost pilgrim-like return to the site of the fire. I decided to follow the old path from my childhood memory. The rains made the going sluggish. Not only was it very wet, slippery, and muddy, the grass and all life forms were heavily laden with water. I was soon soaked right up to my knees. I was glad I had pulled on a pair of comfortable old boots that had heavy rubber soles; I had brought them with me for gardening work.

 After much huffing and puffing, I came upon the burnt-out ruins of my beloved childhood home. The heavy rains over the past couple of days had washed the remains of the house clean. It had done its best to purify it from my uncle's wickedness. The walls glistened white through the early morning mist. The picture of my life's dream flashed through my mind. I had planned it all so very carefully over the years. Now my plans would never materialise. Like a delicate china creation, it was dashed to pieces. The enormity of my loss had now fully registered. It had not been a dream nor was it imagined. Consumed by waves of anguish and the damp chill of the morning, I shivered, mumbled incoherently, and wiped angrily at my eyes. Beset by a sense of hopelessness, I stumbled over unseen objects in my path as I turned away from the centre of the ruins. Angrily, I groped around for whatever I could lay my hands on. Then, in blind rage, I hurled them at the remaining walls of the house and ran away towards the twin hills.

 I paused on top of the hills to catch my breath and gazed unseeing towards the eastern mountains. I watched the sun rising over the tops of the mountains; its light shone brightly as if suspended. It seemed to be denying Peaceful View of its blessed presence. I looked upon the orange red and a sense of gloom clouded my vision. I thought how peculiar life was. Each time I believed I had experienced it all, something came up to knock me face down into the dust. The dark pathways of my memories beckoned me, and I followed and re-lived past experiences as if they were new ones. Purposefully, I willed each memory to come alive as the eerie shadows of the past came back to me. I found myself staring into the face of what troubled my world and threatened my very existence.

The memories were as hauntingly graphic as if they had happened only yesterday. I looked out towards the hills that were once my sanctuary. There I had spent a great deal of my time during my childhood. Then my eyes fell on the family's cemetery. I picked out my grandfathers' tomb and saw the relentless nightmares that used to torment him. It was his reward for fighting for "the mother country". In addition, he had been awarded a medal and a place on a ship that sailed him, dispirited and broken, out of the memory and history of the people and country he was so proud to have served. He had been sent home without one of the two legs he had arrived with. Then, adding insult to injuries, the stump, cut just above his knee, was riddled with gangrene that had not been treated. Although I was born long after the war, I learned the story behind my grandfather's wretched life. He had fought the horrors of a war that, in truth, had nothing to do with him or the Caribbean. Still, as the call for volunteers to fight for the "mother country" swept through the patriotic Caribbean islands like a fever, Grandpa had proudly sailed off into the unknown.

He returned a snivelling wreck. His life revolved around the insignificant things others saw as annoying or tedious. He'd fuss over a missing button from his clothes, or one that had come undone on his shirt. He garbled endlessly about being wet and cold, and Grandma would have to change his clothes to pacify him. This was all part of Grandpa's nightmares, of course, as the war continued in his imagination. Then, one night, Grandma woke me.

"Wake up, Savannah. Grandpa is asking for you."

I cannot recall my age, for I was very young at the time. However; this was my earliest memory of death. Grandma had wiped the sleep from my eyes with the hem of my nightgown and had led me to the bedside she shared with Grandpa.

The whole family had already assembled there. Grandpa had reached out and placed his withered hand on top of my head. He opened his eyes and looked at each of us in turn. His chest made horrible rattling noises and his eyes closed. I was hastily led back to my bedroom and told to remain there. I returned to stand outside Grandma's bedroom door and heard the word "death" spoken. The coldness of Grandpa's hand and the fear of this thing called "death" had sent me running out of the house and into the far reaches of the hills. This was the beginning of my love affair with the hills around Peaceful View. Grandpa's death had set off the trigger that turned into unimaginable nightmares in my world. From here on, the death of loved ones followed in quick succession, and my confusion deepened.

After years of failed operations that had left her speechless and her delicate features horribly disfigured, Aunt Vicky fell asleep in death. Four months after Grandpa died, the cancer that had ravaged her body finally claimed her. Aunt Vicky had fought the debilitating disease bravely. Never once did she complain as it dragged her fighting to the very end. A vision of my aunt drifted through my mind. Her waist-length auburn hair trailed behind her in the breeze. Her ivory skin was pink from the sun, and her pretty face was hidden beneath a straw hat. Aunt Vicky had spent her life as a frail recluse. She was too weak to engage in the family's day-to-day activities and was trapped in a body she could not escape from. No amount of money was spared to send her abroad for treatment, but none of it worked for longer than a few months. In the end, she returned home from her last period of treatment in Canada. The news wasn't good for this time – there was nothing more that could be done for her.

Though I never understood fully what was happening, I had witnessed the sufferings of both my grandfather and my aunt. The memory left a scar that never healed. Aunt Vicky was a truly beautiful and gentle lady who possessed love without reservations. She was tender and sweet and didn't deserve the hopelessness of both her life and her marriage. It was always said, "One as beautiful was not meant for this world; she was surely meant to be an angel." Aunt Victoria's departure sealed my fate. I simply couldn't accept she had gone. My childhood world plunged into one that no longer made sense to me. My world was transformed into one of confusion – an endless merry go round of anger, fear, and guilt. Claude's loathing of me came to light at this time; with each death, his sadistic cruelty intensified. My family's inability to recognize my anguish or the lonely world I inhabited did nothing to help.

Why

When I accidentally set fire to the vestry at our Anglican church, this was seen as deliberate. And when I filled the baptismal fountain with sand and dirt to bury a dead mongoose I had found, Pastor Mac condemned me to hell fire. My troubles didn't end there. I stood on the visiting reverend's robe, and, as he stepped off, his neck was dragged backwards. This sent the paraphernalia in his hands clattering noisily on to the stone floor. But what seemed to be the worst thing I could have done was to be caught digging up my beloved Aunt Vicky in the cemetery at Peaceful View. Pastor Mac pronounced me the devil's child and banished me permanently from church. The unnecessary fears these actions caused and the depths to which I plunged, rendered me unmanageable. I turned into a wild child. At the tender age of eight, I resigned myself to a future of shovelling coal in hell.

CHAPTER 18

I wiped away a tear and gazed into the horizon. From my vantage point, I could see far into the distance and beyond. I stood on top of a formation of rocks that made up the twin hills. The stone I stood on was nicknamed the thinking man stone. Sometimes the spot was called "broken heart graveyard" too. The names of various family members were carved on the surface of the stone. Little love hearts, with Cupid's arrow going through them, were carved next to the names and each had a date. I ran my hand fondly over Uncle Arnold's name; I spelt out each letter with the stroke of my finger. Uncle Arnold had made a name for himself in architecture after his studies in Scotland. When he returned home after obtaining his degree, he married his childhood sweetheart Jane. Their names were entwined in the centre of the largest of the hearts on the stone. Weatherworn now, both writing and carvings had faded with the passage of time. I am sure, though, each had meant something precious to the writer at the time. They related to events – perhaps a marriage, a birth, love, or even the story of a broken heart. The thought of my uncle brought fond memories of him, his infectious laughter, and his wild sense of humour.

The view from this point was particularly breathtaking. The advantages of the spot were many: it was private; you could be sitting here watching the goings on below, and no one would spot you. My uncles, aunts, and cousins used to disappear here to seek solitude or to spend time with their sweethearts away from the glare of our huge family. I suspected promises were made and broken here, and far-reaching decisions that shaped my family's life were taken on this spot. Even Grandma used to come up here. I sometimes caught her crying or talking to herself, and she would forbid me to tell anyone. These are but a few of the memories that made my childhood bittersweet. It was a concealed place to hide away and ponder the twists and turns along the highways of life.

It was my turn now as I sat alone contemplating my life and future. I looked down at the path again. The only visible movements were the swirling white fog that often descended on the island. During the cooler season, and, in particular, when it rained for a while, visibility would be reduced to nothing in the blanket of white. I watched the mist swirling as the wind wrapped itself around it and turned it into a gentle twister. Further into the distance, I could just about see the roof of Aunt Eva's house. The mist blocked the rest of the house from my view. As I brooded over what lay ahead of me, I reached down, ran my fingers through the earth, and wiped away the mud that settled on the only level area on the hills.

Family pets were buried here, and it was Whisky's final resting place too. I brushed the mud away in search of Whisky's little headstone. I found most of the other pets before I finally saw Whisky's name.

"If only you were still alive, Whisky," I said, as I sat with thoughts of a time that still lived on in my memory – a time that held me captive and to which I had been a willing slave.

I had to come to terms with reality again. But this time, I was determined the price wasn't going to be me. I had no desire to be the proverbial sacrificial lamb anymore. The roller-coaster rides of emotions, memories, and experiences flowed. Like water seeking its level, my confidence, anger, and frustration gushed. They dictated my thoughts, which, in turn, pushed me to decisions I must make.

Like some cruel hand shooting a red-hot arrow straight through me, a deep hoarse sound escaped from my throat and a burning pain pierced through my heart. I doubled over clasping my hands to my chest. I sat down, pulled my knees up, and wrapped my arms around them. I rested my chin on top of my knees and waited for the pain to subside. I began to recall a time long ago after Grandpa had died. The sun was in an advanced stage of setting and had cleared the twin hills. Its long journey to the west was nearly over. I had just levelled with the hills, merrily singing a catchy little tune. A sudden need had drawn my eyes upwards to the top of the twin hills. There, on the highest point, stood a strange man I'd not seen before. His unusually dark face looked directly down at me from over the top of the rocks. He was taller than anyone I'd ever seen, and he had bright shiny eyes, which sparkled like diamonds. His small hands rested on his knees, pulling the dress he wore upwards. This revealed his strange horse- like kneecaps. On his head, and leaning slightly to one side, was a broad-brimmed hat in a neutral colour. Bits of haphazardly-trimmed strands of cotton hung from the edges of the hat. He wore shiny black shoes and a pair of short black socks. In addition to the weird feeling his presence caused me, the man was wearing one of Grandma's favourite daytime dresses!

Transfixed, I stared at the semi-crouching figure decked out in Grandma's green-and-cream chambray dress. The cuffed sleeves revealed elbows just like his kneecaps.

"This must be Lucifer," I whispered in a strange gurgle.

A feeling of terror wrapped me up in arms of iron. I was sucked into something chillingly abnormal. I tried to tear my gaze away from him, but I couldn't escape from his sparkling eyes. Then I tried swallowing the saliva that flooded my mouth, but my throat had closed tight. All I could do was blow bubbles and dribble down the front of my clothes. I screamed until my throat felt like flames of fire, but my screams were not heard. They were pulled down into my throat. My voice had altered and all that came out was a croaking sound. Even though I was in visible distance along the path on my way to Aunt Eva's, not a single soul heard my cries or noticed I was in distress. It was as if I had become invisible.

I remembered reaching up to feel my head – it felt swollen. But when I felt it – it was the same normal size. I ran my tongue between my teeth to check its size. For that, too, felt as big and heavy as my head – yet it was still normal. I watched as twilight fell over the twin hills casting orange and gold over the stranger. As his eyes sucked my mind empty of all thought, I blacked out. To this day, not a single member of my family ever mentioned the incident, let alone explaining it to me. Doctor Pitter encouraged me to put the whole thing out of my mind. What, then, had possessed me to come up here today? I wondered. A feeling of uneasiness swept over me now. I glanced behind me, and a mix of raw terror and nausea threw me forward. I felt sick, retched, and then threw up with such force that I toppled face down into the mud.

It was here, on this very spot, that I had witnessed a most hideous and frightening sight that had lay forgotten until now. My skin grew clammy, and I began to sweat profusely. Trickles of water crawled down my back like tiny insects making their way to and fro. I stood up from the pool of mud I had fallen into. Suddenly and without warning, a terrific crack of thunder was followed by fiery flashes of lightening. Electric sparks bounced off the rocks around me, and then struck a tree only yards away. I was sprinkled with flinty pieces of rocks, which cut into my skin. Bits of bark and sap covered me and a shadow closed in over me like a blanket.

I jumped up, and my feet skid down the sloping hills picking out the muddiest and most treacherous way down. I slid, ran, and jumped my way down, crashing into trees and stones alike. My boots were pulled from my feet as if by hand, while I hurtled through thick undergrowth. Sharp objects sliced through the soles of my feet; a branch entangled itself around one of my arms and ripped half my shirt away from my body. There was another enormous crack of thunder, and a tree fell across my path. The ground seemed to slip away from beneath my feet. A mixture of lightening and thunder caused a sugar apple tree directly in front of me to explode, and I was showered again with bark and branches. Stones, mud, and fallen trees were sent rolling down the hillside in hot pursuit of me. I grappled with fear and nature. Predatory branches stretched like hands, which slapped viciously about my body, and ripped the remains of my shirt clean away.

I was catapulted upwards, but I thankfully caught hold of a branch. I prayed it wouldn't snap as I swung my body up and over. Then, as if I was pulled to safety, I landed down onto a level area of ground. In front of me were the final home straits. I charged like a wounded boar around the sharp bend leading to the path and then through the gardens. I ran into a thicket of rose bushes, which seemed to tear my flesh as I fought my way through every possible obstacle. Having made it through the rose bushes, I crashed head on into the silk cotton tree and smashed my face against its huge trunk. Blood oozed from my nose and cut a path down between my breasts. I charged up the steps to the summer house and literally burst through the door.

Like a crazed lunatic, I lunged forward, knocking Uncle Daniel across the floor. Bags fell apart scattering their contents of tins and bottles, which jostled each other for a safe place to hide. Uncle Daniel's little brown dog Sugar looked at me, then cowered in a corner, and covered his eyes with one paw. My body shook in great shudders, and my teeth chattered noisily against each other. I finally came to rest on my knees at a pair of highly polished black brogues. My heart throbbed thunderously, and my muddied tears fell on the brogues. Blobs of mud fell from me and splattered on the floor. My bleeding nose and mouth dripped their contribution to add to the mess in front of me. Muddy and distraught, I crouched in a heap in front of the brogues. I was caught up in a horrifying situation I had no control over, and I broke into sobs.

"I want to go home. I can't take this madness anymore. Someone or something is out to get me… trying to drive me nuts. They or it… is succeeding," I wailed.

A pair of strong arms pulled me up to my feet. My mud-streaked face looked up into enchanting autumn eyes. I saw warmth glowing in his eyes – as if a fire was burning in their depths. His arms closed around me, and I buried my face against his chest. Closing the door on my earlier horrors.

CHAPTER 19

No one spoke. It seemed, Uncle Daniel and Robin were as uneasy as I was, or perhaps, they were too exasperated to speak. Their silence and frequently-exchanged glances riled me somewhat. After all, I hadn't stolen the family silver nor had I done anything to endanger the life of anyone else. I ached all over and felt totally foolish. All I wanted to do was wash away the memory. However, the silence stretched on, and I returned to the hills in my mind's eye. My experience as a child had chased me away from the twin hills, and I became terrified; to even look in that direction. I wouldn't walk past the hills after sunset. Until today, I had very little memory of what happened during my childhood. With Dr Pitter's gentle coaching; I had blanked the whole horrible episode from my mind.

"Savannah… leaving the house this morning without anyone's knowledge was irresponsible under the circumstances," said Robin, breaking the silence at last.

"I agree with Robin," said Uncle Daniel.

My uncle's face was uncompromising, but his voice was soft. Still, I didn't like the look I saw on his face.

"What circumstances? Why was I irresponsible? I only went for a blooming walk!"

"Savannah, last night I asked you to be careful and not to wander off, did I not?"

"Yes, you did. However... you gave me no reason to believe I was to be confined to the house. And anyway, I would not have agreed," I snorted into his chest, and he held me away from him to look down into my face. I resisted and buried my face against his chest again.

"Savannah, have you seen the state of yourself?" His stern voice echoed through his chest and lodged in my ear. I said nothing.

"Your heart's racing out of control. You are covered in blood, not to mention... your muddied state. You look like you've been mauled by a grizzly bear. If your appearance is anything to go by, it appears you are lucky to be alive!"

Robin's feelings erupted, and I did not need anyone to tell me that he was irritated with me. I half expected him to pull the belt from his jeans and give me a hiding for daring to leave the house without permission. Given my going there happened quite unintentionally, not to mention innocently, his sanctimonious attitude gave me a massive dose of the gripes. Anger overrode my earlier terrors now and I exploded.

"Oh, drat... would you credit it. I forgot to walk with my full length mirror this morning. You see, I stop along the way in between my various terrors here - to check my appearance. Robin, do you think I care what I look like right now? I am too busy being grateful to be breathing!"

My words cracked like a whip between us. With his hands on my shoulders, he stepped away from me with disdain. His action caused my muscles to ache; my face felt like a ripe melon. My lower lip looked like a half pound of veal. I was a complete mess both inside and out and didn't care much for the criticisms levelled at me. I shot him a cutting look then went to wipe my face on my shirt. Of course, it had been ripped from my back by handlike branches! I covered my chest with both hands and dashed into the other room. I slammed the door shut with such force that everything in the room shook.

Why

Humiliation and anger caused my eyes to fill up with tears, but I wasn't going to cry. I'd rather drown internally than shed another tear in his presence. I scuttled around hunting for something to hide my embarrassment with and saw a shirt on the back of the door. For a split second, I considered asking permission to borrow it but changed my mind. I put it on and buttoned it up to the neck.

"Savannah, can I come in?" Uncle Daniel was at the door. As much as I wanted to lock myself away, I couldn't say no to Uncle Daniel.

"Yes, you can." I answered sourly.

He stepped into the room and his concerned eyes found mine.

"Savannah, what happened to you? Did someone attack you, princess?"

He sat down and then got up again like he had no idea what to do with himself. Looking even wearier than he had before, he propped up his tall frame against the wall. Robin walked in now, and I had them both to contend with.

"Yes, I was viciously attacked," I answered, hugging the oversized shirt closer to me and trying to understand the bizarre events in the hills.

It was nothing short of abnormal – an almost exact repetition of what happened when I was small except, I didn't actually see the man this time. I was standing on the path at the foot of the hill back then.

"Who attacked you, Savannah?"

The very force of Robin's question made every cut, scratch, and bruise hurt ever harder than before. My huge lip began to throb, and I expected it to pull me down on to the floor with its weight.

"Why do you speak as if it was human?"

"You said so yourself."

"I did not. I said I was attacked. I never said it was by a human being."

"Then what attacked you?"

Having being mauled earlier by every imagined thing nature threw at me; I was now mauled all over again by the force and passion in Robin Pitter's voice. Again I wanted to burst into tears, but I wasn't a weakling. Resilience was something I had been born with, and this man wasn't going to make me quake. I would ignore him.

"Uncle Daniel, it was that thing that caused the lightning and thunder. Landslide, stones exploding trees… the whole kit and caboodle. I was mauled by them all."

I said with impatience, for I did not expect to be believed and would rather put the whole thing out of my head. I wanted to wipe the memory clean, like I had done as a child.

"Exactly where did you get to, Savannah?"

I just wished this man would alter the tone in his voice, for it was winding me up something chronic. Forcefulness wasn't the way to deal with me at all.

"Have I not told you already? It happened in the twin hills. I went there this morning. I became terrified, and then things started happening. Everything just laid into me. Uncle Daniel, have you been here all morning?"

I cast another of my toxic looks in Robin's direction.

"Yes, with the exception of Robin. He was out looking for you."

"Was there a thunderstorm and lightning? Did you see or hear anything?"

"Yes… there was thunder and lightning. It looked like a thunderbolt fell in the hills to the east."

"The… east?" I asked incredulously. "Are you sure it didn't fall on the twin hills to the west?"

"No it was the east… definitely."

Now I wondered if I had gone totally mad. I most certainly did not imagine what happened earlier, anymore than I had imagined it as a child. Something deviant lives in that hill, and I aim to prove it.

"I've seen it, heard it, and lived it. I don't know. I don't understand."

"Why on earth did you go back there?" asked my uncle wide-eyed.

Before I could answer my uncle, Robin laid into me again. The man was like a bear with a sour head.

"Savannah, if you continue to set yourself up as a sitting duck, we will be powerless to protect you. I had you down as level-headed. It seemed… I was wrong!"

"You are both coming at me with guns blazing."

I threw my hands up in dejection.

"What are you protecting me from, for Pete's sake?" I asked crossly.

My uncle and Robin exchanged glances, and I glared from one to the other. The answers I sought were confirmed in their surreptitious glances.

"What possessed you to go back there, Savannah? No one goes there since…"

I tried to purse my lips, but the weight made it impossible. My lower lip was rigid and far too huge to form into anything other than guttering for the tears that had begun to roll down my face. I turned my back on them not because I was rude, but because I wasn't going to give Robin Pitter the satisfaction of seeing me crying again.

"The truth is, my sole purpose this morning was to go to the ruins of the house. I'd forgotten about the twin hills and forgotten about… that thing."

Robin turned and walked out into the other room, and I began to sob now. Uncle Daniel pulled me to him.

"Ouch… my arm. I think it's broken or something."

"Let's get you back to the house. Robin's car is outside. We have to talk to you tonight, Savannah – make you understand. You cannot go off like this again, do you hear?"

Uncle Daniel had never spoken to me this way before, not even when I was a small annoying thorn in his side!

"It's Claude. He's out to get me… isn't he, Uncle Daniel? He wants my head on a platter."

The pained look on Uncle Daniel's face deepened, and his colour drained away. I got off the bed and proceeded to pace the floor. I hated the summer house now, for it had become a place of bad tidings.

Robin returned with a cup and handed it to me. I took the cup and greedily began to guzzle its contents. I soon drained the cup and put it down on the little table under the window.

"Thank you. I needed that."

"Would you like a second cup, Savannah?"

I nodded. There was nothing quite like a cup of tea to calm the nerves and clear the head.

I came to a stop in front of a family photograph on the wall and noticed the only member of the family missing was Claude. He must have been in prison for embezzling something of value from one of the many women he had deceived over the years. Then again, he might have stolen from the family again or been caught with bags of marijuana strapped to his bike. The philandering low life, I thought bitterly. I know I shouldn't harbour feelings of hatred, but I hated him with a passion.

I remembered one particular woman who had turned up at Peaceful View in search of Claude. For some reason or another, most of the family were gathered under the ackee tree in front of the house when someone saw this wretched-looking woman coming up the drive. We all watched her progress, and, as she got closer, giggles broke out because of the strange swinging motion of one of her legs. When she finally stood before us, she had to be given a seat, for the poor woman had been walking since the day before. Once she had been revived with water and a seat under the shade of the ackee tree, she was questioned. Her name was Sissy, and she claimed to be thirty-five years old. Claude had promised her marriage and had persuaded her to hand over her life savings to him. Once he had got his hands on her money, he had vanished into thin air. It had taken her three months to track him down.

Now that she had found his home and family, she was going nowhere! She declared herself Claude's common-law wife until his ring was placed on her finger. In addition, she claimed she was expecting his child. An indignant Grandma felt no pity for her and declared the woman "a sexagenarian". Not only was this woman well past the age of child bearing, she was nearly as old as my grandmother. Sissy was given the money back and sent packing. However, Sissy had other ideas of her own. We soon discovered she had taken up residence in an unused house nearby. The poor deluded woman was in love and hoped Claude would hear of her presence and come looking for her. It never happened, and three months later, she conceded defeat and was seen swinging her bad leg towards the bus station three miles away.

"Uncle Daniel, I'm no fool. I can sense something's in the air, and it reeks of Claude. Am I right?" My uncle nodded rigidly. "So the threat is real then. I mean… what makes you think it's serious. Let's face it. He made this threat before… remember?"

"Why do you think you were sent to England, princess? Mamma never wanted to let you go. It was fear – fear for your safety."

Robin returned with the tea, but I had lost the taste for it; he placed it on the little table.

"Princess, there is something I have to know. It will cause you pain, but I was never sure…"

I placed a finger on my uncle's lips for I knew exactly what it was he wanted to know. A million memories vied for my attention now as I recalled the last time I suffered at Claude's hands.

"I didn't know what was going to happen. I thought he was tying me down to burn me or pee on me or something."

I began to pace again, and my uncle's eyes followed me as I walked the floor. Robin stood in the doorway. He was leaned up against the doorpost and his eyes were focused on a polaroid snap in his hand.

"It was when he called to his friend that I realised something worse than urine or fire, was going to happen to me."

I felt my jaws constricting like they do just before a dentist begins to drill unnecessarily into a perfectly good tooth!

"My clothes were pulled up to my neck. Claude's friend was on top of me. Somehow, don't ask me, for I don't know – but something loosened my legs. I tried desperately to get away and was trashing around when my knee ground into his crotch. He threw himself off me – and doubled up in pain. I screamed and there was Whisky."

"Did this man rape you, Savannah?"

It seemed Robin was in a foul mood and wasn't going to wait for me to compose myself, let alone hear me out.

"No. He didn't actually rape me."

"Actually? Princess?"

I turned around. I wanted to look straight into my uncle's eyes. I wanted him to see the truth in my own eyes and wanted him to forgive himself for what had happened back then. It wasn't his fault he was only protecting me. I picked up the cup of tea Robin had made me and went to sit on the bed. I looked at Uncle Daniel again.

"His friend was bent over me - on his knees. Whisky tore into him, and the flesh just peeled off his arm. He was seen off and he ran back into the bushes… then Whisky turned on Claude."

"You left the island untouched, princess?"

I nodded my head.

In my uncle's old-fashioned way, he wanted to be assured I had left the island an innocent virgin.

Even though the memory was a particularly painful one, I wanted to put my uncle's mind at rest. If I could erase this oppressive guilt and free him from the weight he carried, I had no qualms remembering every minute detail. Thanks to my beloved and faithful dog, I was saved from a fate worse than death. I knew I had confounded the suspicion, for when I had been found wandering around talking to myself, I had refused to tell what had happened. Dr Pitter was called, and he had tenderly tried to coax me into telling him why I was so distressed and why my inner thighs were so badly bruised. Then when he had tried examining me, I had bitten him on his hand, kicked out in fury, and ran away. My secret cave in the eastern hills became a heaven. Here I was safe, and no one but Whisky knew where to find me. This place became known as my second home, for during my frequent disappearance, it was to this place I ran. It was dark, quiet, and very safe. The entrance to the cave was so small, only Whisky and I could squeeze through. Inside, though, it was huge and I had my supplies hidden there. It was shortly after this that I was told by Grandma I would be going to my father in England.

"Uncle Daniel, I left a virgin. I still am."

"Savannah, can you remember who this man was?"

What a Question, I thought. How could I forget his malevolent face? I planned to hunt him down whilst on the island. It was something I had to do.

"Yes. It was Owen."

An indignant sound came up from my uncle's throat. I feared he might be having a heart-attack. I looked to see if he was alright. He gasped and his mouth fell open. His wild staring eyes set Robin off on a path towards me. Robin handed me the polaroid snap he had been studying.

"A mound of earth… ? What's this? Your idea of art?" I retorted, handing the snap back to him.

"Look more closely at the snap, Savannah."

He stood above me with both hands buried deep in his pockets. His face contorted and had turned crimson.

"I've had enough riddles for today. Just tell me what I am supposed to look for."

I thrust the picture at him again.

"It's a grave. Your grave, Savannah!"

I turned my head so suddenly; I felt something snapped in my neck.

"My gr-grave?! I don't understand. What are you saying?"

He handed the picture back to me. I studied it more closely and there it was. A crude memorial plaque written in what looked like red paint and stuck in a mound of freshly dug earth. It read, "Savannah Hanson RIP." The twittering sounds of birdsongs I had heard whilst pacing the floor earlier, died away. Silence descended again, and I realised I had jumped headlong into a fiery furnace of hot passion. It appeared to hold all the answers to the desires that burned inside me and waited to be fulfilled. Life's trickery had other ideas, though, for in just two days, my hopes and dreams transformed beyond anything I could have possibly imagined.

My skin began to crawl, for I had skirted the cemetery earlier when I had set out from Aunt Eva's house. I hadn't seen a soul. But then, the thick mist may have concealed the loathsome imitation of a man. I wondered if I had inherited a curse in place of an estate. That part of me which I disliked – the part that was always too willing to dissolve into an emotional wilderness of denial and despair- beckoned me. Once again, I had to come to terms with the fickle wind of change. If I needed a wake up call, here it was. The poison that had infiltrated my bloodstream when I first saw the burnt-out remains of the house returned. A cold sensation cruised through me. If it wasn't for my heartbeat, which I could clearly feel, I would be easily convinced that something not of this world had wormed its way into my bloodstream.

CHAPTER 20

While I was no stranger to feelings of loneliness, I loathed the anxiety and sense of vulnerability that packed into every space around me. Perhaps it was the awareness of loosing control over a given situation. Whilst I was no control freak, I would rather I had the choice to pick and choose what happened in my life. The present situation not only denied me choice, it denied me my freedom too. I could no longer predict the direction my life would take from one moment to the next. I looked towards where my uncle sat, but there was no change. His countenance registered shock. Had he not been in my presence all this time, I would have thought he had been unfortunate enough to have walked into the ghosts of both Aunt Eva and Aunt Rhonda at the same time. All I wanted to do now was walk, walk, and walk until I ran out of a road to travel down. I wanted to disappear to find a place of solitude but had a feeling that confinement to ugly Aunt Eva's house was what awaited me.

Patricia Barnes

"Daniel, let's get Savannah back to the house."

An animated voice caused Uncle Daniel to walk towards me.

"We must get you back now, Savannah."

Robin walked to the door, and Uncle Daniel stood up and stretched out a hand to me. I pulled myself up, and we walked towards the door where Robin stood waiting. He slid the bolt, turned the key in the lock, and stepped outside. Uncle Daniel followed.

"Wait there until I open the car, Savannah," Robin said.

I waited just inside the door. He went down the steps and into the car. He threw the back door open, and I ran down the steps and darted in. Uncle Daniel slammed the door shut and pulled me down on to his lap. I didn't protest for I was depleted of all vigour. I felt like a small tree when its energy is sucked dry by the summer heat. The car pulled away and slid its way over the grass until it picked up the road leading to Aunt Eva's house. We drove in a sombre hush. Neither Uncle Daniel, Robin, nor I spoke. We all knew the conversation would begin again at Aunt Eva's. The time had come to face the cruelty life often dealt us as a reward for daring to be born. I began to prepare my mind for the revelation of my impending death and the truth that would unravel the mysteries of the fire. My depleted spirit desperately begged to be set free to walk without fear towards a road of recovery. But it wasn't going to be for somewhere in my subconscious; I knew my nightmares had only just began.

Robin drove like a bat out of hell, and we arrived at Aunt Eva's house faster than it had taken us to leave the summer house. He drove straight into the garage in the basement. Uncle Daniel opened a door which took us through a store room, a laundry room, and up a short flight of stairs until we were in the corridor just outside the kitchen. Robin went off towards the sitting room, and Uncle Daniel and I went into the kitchen.

"I'll get us something to eat, and then you can go and freshen up, princess."

I nodded without much thought for my mind was elsewhere.

"Nothing will happen to you as long as there's breath in my body," Uncle Daniel said, as he moved in a flurry around the kitchen.

"Uncle Daniel, please don't worry so much about me. I'm pretty tough, you know. I can take care of myself… you'll see."

"Your disappearing without a word this morning nearly drove me out of my mind. You must promise never to do that again, princess."

How could I make a promise I may not be able to keep? I asked myself. But again, I simply couldn't cause my uncle any more trouble. I was caught between a rock and a hard place.

"OK, I promise."

Promising to do something against my own principles just didn't sit right with me; but if it made my uncle's life a little less fraught, that's how it had to be for the time being. Robin returned just then and stood between the kitchen and the dining room. He looked at me through eyes of autumn fires. He was still clearly angry at me for leaving the house this morning.

"You…" he said, pointing at me.

But then he banished the thought and, instead, ran his hand through his hair. I was about to sit down when his voice boomed at me.

"Savannah, I can't bear to see you looking so unkempt… and Daddy wants to take a look at your injuries."

His word drew my attention to the huge shirt hanging off me. I looked down at myself and had to agree with him. I looked pretty unsightly, not to mention pitiful.

"Yes. I better go and clean myself up," I answered in agreement.

I wasn't going to fight with him when he was so obviously right in his observations. Robin's annoyance drained away for he really wasn't expecting me to have given in so easily. He sat down at the dining table, and I turned and hurried away. I'd rather have a shower, for I, too, was uncomfortable with the mess I had become. The cuts and bruises I had collected needed to be looked at, and it was fortunate that Dr Pitter was there in the house. The soles of my feet throbbed and had a fiery feel to them. I was worried about infection and limped along as fast as I could. I had to cleanse myself of the grime I had collected from the hills. I opened the door to the sitting room and went into my bedroom. There I unfastened my jeans and pulled it off.

My legs were the only part of me without a scratch. I went into the bathroom and locked the door behind me. I headed straight for the bath, climbed in, and stood under the shower. Looking down, I saw a combination of mud and blood around my feet. I ran the water for some time to remove every possible particle of the hills from my body before soaping myself. As the shower gel reached my collection of injuries, my body caught fire. I could have screamed in agony. But, instead, I gritted my teeth and repeated the process time and again until the fire subsided. Next, I washed my hair and stepped squeaky clean from the tub. I wrapped a large towel around myself and went into my room.

I checked my upper body in the mirror and found things wasn't as bad as they had first appeared. The scratches were superficial, apart from a deep cut, about six inches in length, across my midriff. It was an angry red colour, and I gave thanks that I was fortunate to have escaped the worst. The soles of my feet, however, told a different story. I remembered I had brought a first aid kit with me from England. I went through to the sitting room where the boxes were still waiting to be unpacked. With my impending confinement to the house, I would have time enough to empty them and give Uncle Daniel his many presents.

"Whoops…" I gasped.

Robin was sitting there, legs crossed and lips drawn tightly together. He was leaning forward with his elbows resting on his knees and was clearly in deep thought. Next to him on a side table was a pot of coffee. He did not look up, and I was certain he hadn't noticed me standing there. I thought of turning around and going back into my room. But, instead, I hugged the towel tightly and cleared my throat.

"I had no idea anyone was here. I need to get my first aid box from one of those."

I pointed to the fourth box in the middle of the room.

"Let me do that for you, Savannah."

Suddenly he was there beside me, and, for reasons only my perfidious emotions knew, I felt my tear ducts gearing up to cause me additional humiliation.

"It's OK, Robin. I can manage. Thanks."

Then, all of a sudden, he grabbed my hand and pulled me to him. Oh… crumbs, I thought. This wasn't supposed to be happening. I prayed silently and begged my disloyal heart not to let me down. As the temptation to wrap my arms about him urged me on, my practical head took control. I stood with one hand clutching my towel and the other hanging limp at my side. From under the wrap on my head, water began dripping down on to my shoulders. He wiped the water away with his bare hands, and I felt my body tingle one minute and then tense the next. I let out a sigh of air from deep within me, and he set me free.

"How are you feeling, Savannah?"

"I'll live… I dare say. The soles of my feet hurt and my lips tell their own story."

"How did you manage to turn your sweet little face into such a mess, Savannah?"

"Oh… I had a desperate urge to snog a silk cotton tree," I said, and he laughed.

"I admire your sense of humour in the face of such adversity."

"I take it Uncle Daniel failed to tell you… I had been born with nine lives."

"Even with what you're going through here, you still manage to amuse. You amaze me, Savannah."

"That's me – resilience personified. I'm a bit like a rubber ball. Knock me down and I bounce back stronger than before. But don't get any ideas now."

"What's your secret? You intrigue me."

I raised my eyebrows.

"Prayer, faith, reliance on my Creator. That's the source of my strength."

"Umm… the cuts and bruises, Savannah – how did you come by them?"

It seemed he still did not believe I wasn't attacked by human hands.

"I already told you. I was attacked by trees with predatory hands for branches. They slapped me about as if I was a rag doll. It was terrifying. I shan't be going back to that haunted hill again."

"I am delighted to hear that. You had me going out of my mind this morning."

"Why? What am I to you? We aren't even friends. Why are you so worried about me?" Robin looked thoughtfully at me and then strolled over to look out the window.

"Because I feel responsible for you and…"

"And… what?"

He began to rotate his head for a time, and then just when I thought he was going to be doing this forever, he stopped abruptly. He turned leisurely to face me, tilted his head sideways, and looked absorbedly at me. My body tensed and I grew cross.

"Don't feel responsible for me… please. I'm nobody's charity case, and I am more than capable of taking care of myself."

"Umm… I can see that. A good job you're making of it too."

I did not care for his comment or its implications one bit. I frowned at him with narrowed eyes and wondered what it was I had found alluring about him in the first place. Right now, I wanted to stalk up to him and slap his smug face. But without a step ladder or first climbing onto a chair, I'd have difficulty, for he was six feet something and I was five feet one. I banished the thought.

"Once you have finished making yourself presentable, Daddy wants to take a look at you," he said very matter-of-factly.

I nodded and turned towards my bedroom. I locked the door and stood leaning against it for a time. Eventually, I collected myself together and picked out a dress to wear for the evening. I made sure I chose one that would be comfortable against my tender skin. I walked over to the bed with a buttermilk-coloured dress made of soft Indian cotton. It needed no ironing and was loose fitting. In addition, it complemented my complexion and draped beautifully onto my small frame. I was sure the evening was going to be extra chilly, so I took out a sweater and placed it on the back of a chair. I towel dried my hair and teased it into shape. I applied a minimal amount of makeup to conceal the scratches on my face and I looked almost human again. If it wasn't for my fat lips, I would have looked quite lovely. No one looking at me could guess that inside I was dying a thousand deaths all at once.

As I walked to the bedroom door, I hoped my tear ducts wouldn't let me down. I said a prayer, took an extra deep breath, turned the lock, and opened the door. Robin had gone and there were no signs to suggest he was even there. I went straight to the kitchen to find Uncle Daniel, but he wasn't there either. I went back into the corridor and followed the voices I could hear coming from the sitting room. I approached the doorway and stood waiting to catch my uncle's eyes. But, instead, Robin and Mr Stein were the first to notice me. They looked pleasantly surprised, and I lowered my head avoiding direct eye contact. I ached with embarrassment, and the scratches and bruises throbbed as if to remind me. Robin rose to his feet and came towards me. Taking my arm, he led me into the room. I sat down in one of

Aunt Eva's huge armchairs and was soon elbow deep in the soft comfort of rich beige and cream damask. Uncle Daniel turned soulful eyes on me, and I winked at him with pretended gusto.

Through the window in front of me, I noticed a golden hue had already skimmed the clouds over the mountain towards the west. I shifted my eyes away from that direction and sank further into the chair. I sat, not quite happy, but not overly sad either. I would have to get used to this or find something to fill my days. I expected I would bake, cook, and sew. I enjoyed these pursuits. Until I escaped again, I would have to make my confinement as creative as I possibly could. Otherwise, I would go insane.

"Savannah, my dear, you appear to have got over your ordeal?"

"I'm alright, apart from my feet and a cut on my tummy, that is."

I attempted to part my lips into a smile, but the tightness warned me not to. I winked instead.

"Let me have a look at your feet, dear."

Dr Pitter knelt down in front of me, and I lifted one foot on to his knee. He tapped the other foot, and I did the same again.

"Let's get you on your back, my dear, so I can have a better look."

That mischievous side of me smiled. I raised an eyebrow at my darling friend, and he blushed a deep red. I stood up and slid my arm into his. We left the sitting room, and I limped back to my bedroom supported by the surprisingly strong arms of this wonderful man I loved dearly.

I went straight to the bed and lay across it with my feet hanging over the side. Dr Pitter went to the dresser and picked up the little stool in front of it. He sat down, and I lifted my feet onto his lap. He prodded and poked around for sometime while I ouch'd, aaah'd, and winced whenever he touched a tender spot. There was a knock on the door.

"In you come, son." I figured he must be talking to Robin. Who else would Dr Pitter be calling son? "Thank you. Now open it and put it on the bed for me."

Robin had brought the huge black bag Dr Pitter always travelled with in case of an emergency. It crossed my mind Dr Pitter must have seen this coming when he heard I was back at Peaceful View. He had been called out to me as a child so many times that I couldn't count them if I tried.

"I can't watch this…" I heard Robin say.

I almost called him a big girl's blouse for being a coward. After all, wasn't he supposed to be a man? With this acknowledgement, and right on cue, my tummy began to protest with hunger. As if adding to my already defenceless state, my tummy rolled like the thunder that had me running from the twin hills. As a child, I was terrified of thunder and still was. In order to pacify me during my moments of knicker-wetting terror, Grandma used to tell me it wasn't thunder but angels rearranging heavy celestial pieces of furniture across the glassy floors of the heavens. Right now, those divine creatures had turned their attention on my hungry belly. Embarrassed, I closed my eyes and shut the figure of Robin Pitter out.

"Savannah, my dear, you are still as brave as you were the day I first bumped into you."

"Oh… I wouldn't bet on that, Dr Pitter. If you carry on poking around… I will burst into tears."

"That's a bit late considering I have finished."

"Finished?" I asked.

It seemed my brief observation of Robin had taken my mind away from my feet.

"Yes. Finished. I have removed all particles of gravel and dirt from your wounds. You will feel discomfort for a while, and then it will settle down. Now, turn over and let me see that thunderous tum of yours."

I rolled over on to my back and stole a peek in the direction I believed Robin to be. As if sensing this, his eyes met mine. I had to take my mind off my aching feet for the pressure Dr Pitter had exerted left my feet throbbing right up to my knees. I shot Robin one of my "scoot" eye signals for he had served his purpose and no way was I going to lift my dress up with him in the room. He shifted and looked at the door but did not move. I screwed up my eyes like a snake and peered more menacingly at him.

"I better leave you to it. I will be in the sitting room if I am needed," he said.

He closed the door, and I raised one leg into the air. To my dismay, my foot was padded with gauze and a layer of bandage was wrapped around it in a perfect figure of eight. I raised the other.

"Crumbs! I can't walk on these. They will get dirty and infected in no time."

"I don't expect you to walk, my dear. There are five men in the house. I expect we will be cueing up at your command," Dr Pitter chuckled to himself.

I lifted my dress up under my chin and watched Dr Pitter's face as he looked at my tummy. The warmth in his fading blue eyes bathed the ugly cut on my skin. I prepared for him to tell me, he would have to stitch me up. As a little girl, I had seen this look on his face on numerous occasions when he had comforted me or talked my fears away. I trusted him implicitly. I would, if necessary, allow him to stitch me up without anaesthetics.

"Savannah, my dear, I don't like the look of this at all."

Was I surprised? No, for it was a nasty-looking wound. If I had shown it to Uncle Daniel or Robin, neither one would believe it wasn't the result of a sharp blade instead of branches.

"Dr Pitter, I don't want anyone to know about this. Promise me you won't say a word… please."

He adjusted his glasses and stood up.

"I am sure you have a valid reason, my dear. But I am not comfortable with this at all."

"I want Uncle Daniel and Robin to go to that blooming hill and see for themselves… I wasn't attacked by a human being. They will see the stones and whatever else it was that had tried to kill me. It was a supernatural thing, you know."

"Alright. But tomorrow you must allow me to take you to the clinic. You will be one of the first patients and will be safe from all harm there."

Dr Pitter made no comment in relation to what had happened earlier in the hills, and I wondered whether arrangements had been made to take me off to a lunatic asylum!

"Let me patch you up now. Tomorrow, first light, I am taking you to Montego Bay."

As much as I respected, loved, and trusted Dr Pitter, he was going to make this journey on his own. A neat little plan, it seemed, had been hatched without my knowledge. But I would just have to derail it. My promise to Uncle Daniel melted like a lump of ice left in the sun.

Tonight, I was going to snatch control of my life back from under their very noses. But first, I would be the optimum of grace and charm. I was going to exude such inner peace that none of them would suspect

I would be gone long before they drifted off into their individual world of sleep. The evil Pastor Mac was dead and not a moment too soon. But it seemed his prediction lived on in the minds of those I trusted the most. If they – meaning my uncle, Dr Pitter, Robin, and Mr Stein – believed I was mad, they hadn't seen madness yet. I had no intention, whatsoever, of being taken to Montego Bay or anywhere else for that matter.

CHAPTER 21

A little stouter around the middle now, and a bit older and wiser, he was still as special to me as he was when I was a child. With eyes of empathy and hands of both skill and tenderness, Dr Pitter proved to be my human saviour once again. I loved him to bits, and the love in my heart stirred my tear ducts; the capricious things threatened to turn me into a weeping nuisance. I held my tears back and forced my fat lips into a smile.

"How do I thank you, Dr Pitter?" I asked, looking up into those reassuring eyes that dripped kindness down at me.

"You have done that, my dear. For years I have thought about you a thousand times and looked hopefully to the future on your behalf. I get to see you again before I also… join my beloved wife and friends. I still miss them, you know."

His tender eyes misted up, and I took his hands and kissed them both; they had treated me with the utmost care over the years. There were no words to express the thanks they deserved, but I would try to say what I felt in my heart.

"Thank you for all you did for me as a child. Thank you for being here for me now and thank God for allowing us to be together."

Tears welled up in both our eyes, and he hugged me to him.

"You've blossomed into a very attractive young woman, Savannah. I couldn't be happier if you were my own daughter."

I buried my head into his arms for tonight was perhaps the last time I was ever going to see him again. I would remember this moment forever; my arms tightened around his waist. I was truly grateful this special man had not died as my imagination would have me believe. In spite of whatever was planned for me, I was exceedingly blessed to have known him.

"Let's go and join the others," I said, grabbing his hand and pulling him to the door. With our arms tightly entwined, I limped happily to the dining room.

On our way back, Dr Pitter suggested I sit there for he was famished and was going to order Uncle Daniel to put supper on the table. As I made myself comfortable, I realised I had not seen Bobby at all. I wondered where he had got to.

"How are you feeling, princess?"

I turned my head to see Uncle Daniel was behind me along with Dr Pitter, Robin, and Mr Stein.

"I'm fine, Uncle Daniel. Dr Pitter sorted me out and forbid me to leave the house."

That wasn't quite true, for Dr Pitter did nothing of the kind. But I knew Uncle Daniel would buy it and would sleep easy without worrying I was going to abscond in the middle of the night. He looked down at my bandaged feet, and a glimmer of a smile passed over his face. I supposed he was relieved to see my feet swathed in yards of cloth, for it was added surety, I would be going nowhere. I willed the swollen mound that had replaced my lips into a broad grin even though I was positive that I looked hideous and that my lips resembled a couple of steaks.

"What a transformation from the human mud heap I saw earlier."

It was a no-holds-barred observation delivered with complete innocence. We had no choice but to laugh ourselves to tears – at Mr

Stein's remark. Any tension that had remained in us was laughed right out the window, and I almost whooped for joy.

"Savannah, you look so much better and that colour has put the sparks back into your eyes."

"How very poetic, Robin. Thank you."

Even the usual tension between us got the hint and wandered off into the dusk. He came to sit beside me and Uncle Daniel, Dr Pitter, and Mr Stein shepherded themselves into the kitchen.

"I meant that… I am delighted to see that spark has returned."

"Careful. I wouldn't get too close for those very sparks… might just send you up in a puff of smoke."

I smiled a honey dripping smile at him – in spite of my rubber-lips.

"Young lady, you can scorch me anytime you like."

Flipping Norah, I thought! On which ocean was his boat floating? What on earth was going on in his head? I wondered. Then I caught the faintest whiff of brandy on his breath.

Umm - brandy talk. I thought.

"Get lost. Your breath smells like a brewer's backyard."

I shifted on the chair like I was dismayed by him. But, of course, I wasn't, for he most certainly did not smell like a brewer's backyard. In fact he smelled quite delicious, and I discretely sniffed on the air around us. I would have loved to nuzzle his neck but restrained myself for I was in enough trouble and had no plans to sink any deeper.

"Have I told you, Savannah, you look especially beautiful tonight?"

This man was definitely on something. Considering he made no such compliment prior to me snogging the silk cotton tree, I wondered whether he was for real! I leaned forward and peered into his eyes.

"Robin, do you have a handkerchief?"

"Yes. Do you wish to borrow it?"

For a moment I could see Martin sitting beside me instead of Robin, and this drew my eyes to Robin's hands. I waited for him to give me his handkerchief with a condition attached.

"Yes, please. Could I?"

He fished around in his pocket and passed me his handkerchief. I stared at it for a while. It was a nice enough handkerchief, but it didn't look or smell like Martin's. I heaved a sigh, for I suddenly remembered I still hadn't got the chance to call Martin. I registered this in my memory and peered into Robin's eyes again. I reached up, and, with a single finger; I drew his face closer to mine. The cheeky beggar puckered up in anticipation of a kiss! As if the handkerchief were the palm of my hand, I slapped him across his puckered lips.

"Do you think I was going to kiss you?" I asked.

"Why, yes! I expected you to kiss me."

He even had the nerve to admit it! Bare-face cheek, I thought.

"You have more nerve than a wisdom tooth. Do you often take advantage of defenceless women?"

"Certainly not. And you…" he said with emphasis, "… are far from defenceless. In fact, I've not met one so small with such mettle. Why… you're a little fireball."

"Ok. Here's why I wanted your blooming hanky. I was going to use it to clear whatever it is that's hampering your vision." With this, he looked as though I had managed to confuse him. "You said earlier – and I quote – 'you look beautiful tonight'. You see, Robin, apart from the dress I'm wearing - I feel nothing near beautiful. I think you are taking the Mick because I look like I've accidentally walked into a boxer's glove."

"Savannah, you are riddled with suspicions. It doesn't become you," he said with a proud curl to his lips.

Haughty brute, I thought.

"Tonight, I feel awfully benevolent. I refuse to take on your insults for I happen to know… you mean none of them. You are simply on a facetious role."

"You are right. I won't fight with you tonight. I'll save it for another time."

"Good idea."

He got up and excused himself, and I rolled my eyes. I had already figured out he was easily offended and was just amusing myself. I figured he was still as spoilt as he was when he wore short trousers. Uncle Daniel, Dr Pitter, and Mr Stein began ferrying food to the table, and Robin returned with a glass of brandy in hand perhaps to soothe his bruised ego. I looked at him under my eyelashes and thought of saying something, but I had toyed enough with him for one night. I decided against it. I'd leave him to enjoy his brandy for now. Later, if the mood took my fancy, I'd torment him a little more.

"What are we having tonight, Uncle Daniel?" I asked, as he placed a plate in front of me.

Dr Pitter brought a platter with crispy fried sardines and chunky slices of bread to the table, and the question of dinner was duly answered. I had promised Uncle Daniel I would take over the cooking, but here I was waited on by him and all because I had gone back to that place where demons dwelt in disguise.

The platter was passed from hand to hand around the table, and we helped ourselves to as much or as little as we felt able to eat. I bowed my head in my own silent prayer of thanks and noticed everyone followed suit.

"Uncle Daniel, where's Bobby?" I asked the minute I had said amen.

No one had made mention of Bobby, and there were still no signs of him. The weather was still unrelenting, so I couldn't figure out why I had not seen him.

"He left at first light to see about the drawings for his future home."

"Crumbs! He works fast. Did he say where exactly he was going?"

"Mandeville, I believe. His lady friend lives there. He might not be home tonight."

"He is wasting no time in getting started."

"I take it your feet have settled down, Savannah, my dear?"

The question took me by surprise, for, suddenly, the subject had switched back to me. I looked down the length of the table to where Dr Pitter sat.

"They are feeling better… a little hot, though. Thank you."

"I will loosen the bandages before bedtime. It might be wise to allow air to get to the wounds."

I'd better steer the conversation away from myself again.

"Princess, I like that dress you are wearing."

Before I could explore other lines of communication, Uncle Daniel got to the touch line first.

"You don't look so bad yourself," I replied straightening his collar.

"Umm… you smell good," I said, catching a scent wafting up from his shirt.

He studied me for a split second, and I wondered whether he was able to read my thoughts through my eyes. I turned away and picked up another sardine, which was going down a treat with Uncle Daniel's pickled vegetables. Before long, we had polished off the remaining crumbs from the platter. I decided I would definitely be adding fried sardines to my recipe collection. They were delicious and very nutritious too. I hadn't eaten them since my childhood and had forgotten how very palatable they were.

With what felt like a hideous smile on my face, I glanced around the table. It seemed no one wanted to talk much tonight. Mr Stein hadn't said a single word. However, whenever our eyes met, I got that meaningful look of his, which worried me. Something was definitely bubbling gently between them. I could feel it in my aching bones.

"We have soup to follow, princess. You don't mind having it again so soon, do you?"

"No. We are having soup weather anyway, and I do love soup."

Everyone was obviously hungry for they got up from the table and rushed straight to the sideboard. Robin had picked up my bowl, so I remained seated. My feet would have made the journey back- a very shaky one anyway. My thoughts turned back to Bobby. I wondered why he had not mentioned his plans to me. On the other hand, I was far too busy being chased from the twin hills. Nonetheless, he could have mentioned it last night. I thought of finding out more when the telephone down the hall began to ring.

"Shall I get that, Daniel?" Robin asked, as he placed my bowl of soup in front of me.

"Yes, please, Rob."

Robin hurried down the hall, and everyone sat down to await his return. My bowl of pumpkin soup glistened in front of me, and I ached to taste it. I too made an absolutely divine pumpkin soup. I didn't have to wait too long, for Robin returned and sat down at the table again. Uncle Daniel looked enquiringly at him.

"It was a call for you, Savannah. A Martin Hamilton calling from London."

I rotated my shoulders in delight as my spirits lit up like a light being switched on. I beamed at everyone. I could have clapped my hands in glee for I couldn't have heard a better sound. I stood up; my pumpkin soup could wait until after I had spoken to darling Martin.

"I told him we are having supper. He will call you back at eight."

Why

I checked my watch. Six forty. I had arrived on a Wednesday so it must be Friday today. I realised I had lost track of the days. I ate my soup in haste counting the minutes down with every spoonful.

"Who is Martin Hamilton, Savannah?" Robin asked.

I guess curiosity had got the better of him. I waited to see if Uncle Daniel was going to join in the conversation. But he left me to it.

"Oh... he's a friend. We worked together until recently."

"Uncle Daniel, I will do the washing up after supper," I announced, changing the subject.

"I think you should rest your feet for a while, princess. Us men can deal with the dishes. You go and wait for your call."

I pushed my soup bowl aside and patted my protruding tummy taking care not to touch the ugly cut across my middle. Robin began clearing the table, and I excused myself from their company.

I limped my way to the bathroom near Aunt Eva's former bedroom. From there, I planned to go straight to the sitting room and wait by the telephone. I flossed my teeth, rinsed my mouth with Listerine, and smoothed a light coating of Vaseline over my jumbo lips. The men were still loitering around in the dining area as I passed by - on my way to the sitting room. I went in, sat down in the armchair opposite the window, and looked at the telephone. Nothing happened, but I would wait for Martin's call if it took all night. I wished, though, I had picked up a book; I would like nothing better than to loose myself in a good read. I could hardly contain myself for I longed to hear Martin's reassuring voice and dry wit. I couldn't wait to tell him all that had been happening to me since arriving home. I could see his face clear across the miles of water that separated us - when I tell him; I had a crazed uncle who not only wanted me dead. He had already dug my grave in preparation of my burial.

My excitement mounted as I waited. But the feeling was swiftly thwarted for I was seized with an acute sense of danger. I couldn't put in plain words the sensation that came over me. I felt the blood drain away from my face, my senses sharpened, and a wax-tight feeling replaced the face I sat with moments ago. An overwhelming urge to hurry from the room caused me to stand up from the chair. Then a feeling of approaching danger from the direction of the window drew my eyes there. My heart thumped madly, and I pressed my hands to my chest to quieten my heart. I peered through the gap between the curtains. Pressed up against the glass was one venomous eye all red in colour. With an infusion of wickedness, the eye homed in on me from between the gaps in the curtains. I felt faint and stumbled backwards but managed to remain on my feet.

Like a laser beam, the red eye found me. Before I had a chance to run from the room, there was a frenzied cry of pure lunacy followed by an earth-shattering sound of breaking glass. Something dreadfully hard slammed into my head, and I was sent careering backwards. I grabbed on to the drinks trolley to steady myself, but the force of the blow dragged both the trolley and me along until the trolley overturned. A burning sensation rippled through my upper arm, and I collapsed in a crumpled heap against a wall. I had no idea what it was that had slammed so viciously into the side of my head, neither had I seen anything other than the eye. I touched my head and saw blood on my hands in addition to that dripping from my left arm. I looked down at my beautiful dress in sadness.

"Oh… my lovely dress will be ruined," I wailed.

I tried to save it, but it was no use. My nose too dripped a deep red down the front of it. I was despairing at the thought I may have to throw my dress away, when bells began ringing like wailing sirens in my aching head. The burning sensation in my arm heightened the pain in my head. I looked to see what was causing this burning and saw a shard of glass had embedded itself in my upper arm. I tried to extract it but began to loose control of my awareness. I couldn't keep my hand steady enough to extract the glass. I leaned back on the wall and rested my head there. I became acutely aware that should I surrender to the overwhelming need to lay my aching head down, I may never wake up again.

Oddly I felt no fear – just a calm assurance in the force that guided me. My eyes began to close and my mind wondered as if spirited away. I found myself in what used to be Grandma's beautiful garden. It was peaceful and very quiet. The only sound I could hear was a gentle fluttering that drew my eyes up above my head. In the branches of the avocado tree, pretty and vividly-coloured humming birds shimmered their tightly-packed feathers over me. They hovered on the breeze a while and then whizzed around and formed a canopy above my head. The tips of their long streamer-like tails swept lightly over the top of my head, and the pain eased a while. I tried to catch the hummingbirds, but they eluded me every time. When I opened my eyes again, the picture melted away and the pain returned again. A fresh sensation of burning rushed through me again. I opened my eyes to see Robin removing the glass from my arm. The burning was replaced by numbness. I felt nothing now.

Uncle Daniel placed something on my head and Robin helped me up. He led me through the chaos of glass and bits of window frames to my bedroom. How extraordinary! I thought, for when I had first set eyes on him, I had boldly created this very scene in my mind. Of course, the circumstances were of a romantic nature. I had imagined it was our honeymoon and neither my arm nor my head had hurt. The only ache I had experienced was my imagined anticipation for him. I was aware of everything around me, yet I felt unconnected to it all. I was some place else watching the proceedings from a distance. Perspiration and coldness enveloped me now, and my thoughts came and went. I seemed to be hovering between two worlds. Visions of my childhood pulled me one way, while the present and my uncle's safety, pulled me in another. The pain grew more absorbing and a pressing agony raged deep in my brain. I closed my eyes again, but something wet was slapped on to my face. It disturbed the calmness I felt – for I was in Grandma's garden.

Aunt Victoria, Grandma, Aunt Rebecca, Grandpa, Uncle Arnold, and Dick were all there waiting for me. I knew other aunts and uncles I couldn't see were there also. They were all waiting for me; I could hear their voices calling to me as I walked through the garden and towards them. The hummingbirds hovered over me, and I chased after them as they flew towards Grandma and her open arms. I waved excitedly to everyone as I ran towards my grandmother. It was my welcome home party. I was home at last on my beloved island of Jamaica.